The Making of Fingers Finnigan

Things were changing. First there was the pool campaign. Weird George started it, of all people. Julie and Bee found him clearing the pool up, spadeful by spadeful of sand into old carrier bags.

Then there was Fingers. They all met him in such unusual circumstances that Robert mistook him for his guardian angel, while Bee and Julie privately thought he was a wailing banshee. Actually he was just a boy in trouble, but it took a while to sort that one out.

Unexpectedly the two discoveries merged into a single triumphant finale. To everyone's amazement the pool was re-opened; and as for Fingers – he was made!

How Green You Are, another book about the same group of kids, is also available in Fontana Lions.

BERLIE DOHERTY

The Making of Fingers Finnigan

Fontana Lions

First published in Great Britain 1983
by Methuen Children's Books Ltd
First published in Fontana Lions 1985
by William Collins Sons & Co Ltd
8 Grafton Street, London W1

Text copyright © 1983 Berlie Doherty
Illustrations copyright © 1983 John Haysom

Printed in Great Britain by
William Collins Sons & Co Ltd, Glasgow

'Finnigan's Angel and the Saturday Matinée'
was broadcast on Radio 4's Morning Story
as 'Finnigan's Angel'.

Conditions of Sale
This book is sold subject to the condition
that it shall not, by way of trade or otherwise,
be lent, re-sold, hired out or otherwise circulated
without the publisher's prior consent in any form of
binding or cover other than that in which it is
published and without a similar condition
including this condition being imposed
on the subsequent purchaser.

East Lothian
District Library

WITHDRAWN

JF
DON

Contents

For my mother and father, Peggy and Walter

1 · The Swimming Pool Campaign

I can well remember the day it started. It was Saint Swithin's Day, and it was raining. Someone in the paper shop told me that if it rained on Saint Swithin's Day it would rain for forty days and forty nights afterwards, and as I shoved my last soggy *Liverpool Echo* through my last streaming letter-box I wondered if it had rained on any other Saint Swithin's Day that I could remember, and whether it would be like this, chucking it down every day, or whether a little spatter when the tide was turning would count. We certainly needed something to cheer us up. It was the most miserable summer I could ever remember.

Then I saw Weird George, wobbling down the road on his bike. Weird George lives in our street, next to my friend Julie's. He's the sort of boy that some people make fun of and shout names at in the school-yard; and other kids avoid like the plague because he doesn't fit in with them. I quite like him, really. I suppose I've got used to him. I couldn't understand what he was doing down the posh part, though; he never comes this far as a rule.

I came out of the drive and waved at him, hoping the surprise of it wouldn't make him fall off his bike.

'Where you going, George?' I shouted.

He looked as if he'd rather pretend he hadn't seen me.

'Baths,' he said to the other side of the road, and wobbled off towards the prom. That's the sad thing about George. You just get to the point of thinking he's all right, really, he's just like everybody else, when he goes and does a soft thing like that. Not only was it a daft day to be going swimming in an open-air pool – but everyone knew it had been closed down since the end of last summer. The council had had enough of it.

I followed George down the road, but I had to push my bike. The rain was coming in slices rather than drops, pouring off the hood of my duffle-coat and down my face and inside my blouse-collar. It could have been coming right down the inside of my coat for all I knew, and out the other end. My jeans were soaked anyway.

It was high tide. Huge grey waves slapped against the sea walls and nosed across the pavements the length of the prom. The gutters were high with rain water, so if you closed your eyes it looked as if the tide had come right over the wall and across the pavement and over the road to the houses at the other side, and the cars sloshing down the road were really driving through the sea.

The baths were built out from the sea wall and onto the sand; white, like a Moorish temple. I've never seen anything like it except in travel books, and it was definitely the nicest building for miles around. It looked beautiful when the sun was shining on it. On hot days you could lie out on the white slabbed sunbathing area, like cats in the sunshine, or you could go up onto the balcony and look out over the sea at the little black boats and pretend you were defending the town against all invaders. You could wave at all the daft people splashing about in the gritty brown sea and then run down and plunge into the peppermint green baths water with music wafting out of the loudspeakers and cups of hot Bovril waiting for you in the cafeteria. You could spend all day there, swimming, sunbathing, swimming again, till by the time you went home your skin was wrinkled like an old shrimp and your shoulders were blazing with sunburn.

And then the council decided to shut it down because it wasn't paying. 'It's a waste of time, that place,' the grown-ups grumbled. 'It's all right on a stinking hot day.'

All right! It was the best place in the world.

Now it looked freakish, bravely white and Moorish still, the door boarded up, the gates loaded with sandbags, details of last summer's gala peeling off like old wallpaper. The whole length of the promenade was deserted, but sure enough, George's bike was propped up against one of the benches. Was he inside the baths? I had a vision of him swimming all alone up and down the pool, with rainwater plopping like bursting blisters all around him.

'George!' I shouted. 'Are you in there?' Having followed him down, I felt responsible for him. I could hardly hear myself for the rain thundering down from the ledge of the building into the pools and swilling by the benches, but I felt sure I could hear something that

9

sounded very much like a sneeze, and then another, and George's voice floating through. ... 'Atishoo! Atishoo! Ah! Bless me!'

But I was too wet to be bothered to wait around any more. I wheeled my bike back home through the puddles, knowing my mum would make me a bowl of hot soup and shout at me and find me a big warm towel to dry myself with.

It's funny how being out in the rain makes you tired. By the time I'd finished off two plates of stew I could hardly keep my eyes open, so I found myself a book to read and went off to bed. The sky was greyer than ever, getting ready for night-time darkness. I went to draw my curtains and looked out onto the wet street, gleaming in the yellow lamp-light. Someone was cycling up from the posh part. I watched the hunched figure skim down through the rippling pools, and stop at the house over the road from mine. It was Weird George, wet as a rat, and before I closed my curtains I saw the light come on in his passage and heard his mother's voice, raised in anger. He was in for it then.

Next day was just as bad. Even so Julie and I escaped out into the rain, because we'd both found out that as long as we were in our houses, our mums would find us something to do. We headed down for the prom; we always did. There wasn't anywhere else, really, except up and down the main road, and we did that on Saturdays.

There were a few people on the beach, braving the weather; kids with Wellies on, stomping in the mud. Dads looking bored. There wasn't even an ice-cream van on the prom. But there was Weird George's bike, in exactly the same place as it had been yesterday, and without a combination lock on it. George used to be so proud of that bike. He tried to bring it into the classroom once, so it wouldn't get pinched. And there it was, just lying round for anyone to take.

'He must be daft,' I said.

'He is,' said Julie.

But she wouldn't believe me that he was actually inside the baths. There was no way in, for a start. We walked all the way round it. All the doors were very firmly boarded up.

'But he is in there, I know it.' I said. I cupped my hands round my mouth and yelled at the top of my voice, 'George! Are you in there?'

No reply. Julie looked triumphant.

'What you doing, George?' I shouted again.

And back came his voice, thin as an echo. ... 'Nothing. ... '

'Right,' I said to Julie. 'There's only one way he could have got in, and that's over the top. Are you coming?'

We went round to where his bike was parked. It was just below a sort of overhang parapet, firmly wedged between some benches and a support pillar. He must have climbed up his bike and scrambled up from there, there was no other way. I climbed onto the bench and steadied myself with one foot on the saddle and one on the bench top. It wasn't easy, even with Julie holding the bike. Then I gripped the parapet ledge and swung myself onto it. It took three goes, and I grazed my knees every time. When I was at last standing on the parapet I could see that the next stage, clambering up over the top and on to the inner balcony that overlooked the pool, was going to be comparatively easy.

'Come on, Julie.' I called.

'I think I'd better stay and look after his bike,' she said.

It wasn't a bad excuse but I wasn't going to let her get away with it. 'Look in the saddle-bag,' I ordered. 'See if he's left the combination lock in there.' I could hear her rummaging away but I didn't dare look down in case I fell off.

'Nothing here,' she called up at last. 'Only loads of carrier bags.'

I thought perhaps she better had stay with the bike. I couldn't imagine how I was going to get down without her help, anyway. There were some air-vents from the cafe about half-way up the next wall, and by lodging one foot in them and scrabbling at the top ledge with my hands I managed to heave myself up over the top, and jump down to the balcony. Then I ran across and leaned over the rail to look down at the pool.

It was desolate, like a football stadium when all the crowd's gone home. The pool was about ankle-deep in brown sludgy water, and there were drifts of sand in all four corners.

And there, in the middle of it all, was Weird George.

He was squatting in the damp sand, and scooping out handfuls of it to tip into a bulging carrier bag. He worked mechanically, swaying his body from side to side. He never looked up. He seemed lost in concentration. I watched him sadly. He was like a little boy, I thought, playing in the sand. Why had he taken all this trouble, risking his neck and his precious bike to climb in here, when there were miles and miles of soggy sand on the beach for him to play with?

Suddenly he jerked himself upright – I could hear his knees clicking themselves back into place even from where I stood – grabbed hold of his carrier bag and dashed up out of the swimming-pool, across the sunbathing area, and up the steps opposite me onto the balcony. I crept up on him. The wind was blowing towards me so although I could hear him sneezing and muttering away to himself he couldn't hear me coming. He jumped like a startled rabbit when he saw me, then he swung his loaded carrier bag over the side of the baths, tipped it up, and emptied the lumps of wet sand onto the beach below.

He smiled happily.

'Twenty-five!' he said.

I followed him down the steps and back to his muddy pool. His gym shoes squelched with every step he took, and mud oozed over the tops and through the holes where his big toes poked through. He stepped straight in again and squelched over to where he'd been squatting before. Scoop by scoop he put handfuls of mud into his collapsed carrier-bag.

'George,' I said gently from the side. 'What you doing?'

'Busy working,' he answered, without looking up.

I watched helplessly. I heard Julie tinkling the bicycle bell outside and realised it was nearly time for me to

go on my paper-round. I stood up reluctantly. I didn't like to leave him there.

'Why don't you come and play on the beach, George?'

He snorted in annoyance, and pushed a muddy hand across his hair. 'I'm not playing, I'm working!' he shouted. 'Can't you see? I've got all this here sand to get out. It's a lot of work, this is. You don't offer to help, do you? It's hard work, this . . . '

'But why d'you want to get all the sand out, George? There's tons of it!'

He considered me slowly. 'Because I want to swim, that's why. You can't swim in sand, can you?'

'But George . . . ' He was burrowing away again furiously, dog-like. 'We couldn't swim here anyway. They've closed it down.'

He sighed. 'They can always open it up again, can't they?'

I stared at him. We'd all been shocked and furious when we'd heard the council were closing down the open-air pool, but not any of us had thought of doing anything about it. I thought of my mum, shouting at the television last budget day . . . 'That's the trouble with this country,' she'd said. 'We all grumble, but we don't do anything to put things right. We take things lying down, all of us . . . '

She was right. Nobody but George would have thought of trying to make the council change their minds. It was too silly for any of us to think of. But it could work. They certainly weren't going to change their minds if they thought nobody was bothered anyway.

The bicycle bell was jangling again. You'd have

thought the beach was on fire, the row she was making. 'I'll have to go, George,' I said. 'But I'll try and get some of the others to help. Would you like that?'

But he was absorbed in his digging again, and seemed to have forgotten all about me.

I walked slowly up the steps and along the balcony to the parapet, but when I came to swing myself over I heard Julie's voice raised in argument. I peered over the top. Holding on to George's bike was Julie's favourite enemy, the nosiest girl in our street, Marie Wood. She's like her mother. She's got a mouth like a letter-box that's never shut, and a nose like a vacuum cleaner, sniffing up everything in sight. And standing on the other side, so he could admire Julie from a distance, was her second favourite enemy, Marie's brother Andrew. He's like a lamp-post, that lad. He's taller than any man in our street, and he's got broad, flat feet like kippers. He's like a cross between a stick insect and a frog. And his ears stick out. I can't stand him. He spends hours outside Julie's house, pretending not to look through her window, looking for all the world like a clothes prop that's lost its line. He's soppy. I was glad it was Julie he was after, and not me.

I dodged back down again, trying to decide what to do. The last person I wanted to meet on a wet day was Marie Wood, especially if I had to ask her to catch my legs for me as I came down. And I certainly wasn't going to invite her in to help poor old George with his pool – he hadn't done anything to deserve that! And I didn't want her making silly remarks like 'What you doing in there with George Nightingale, Bee Horton? Can't you find anyone better than him to take you on?' She would, she says things like that.

No, the best thing I could do was to wait until I was quite sure she'd gone. I tucked myself down against the side and chewed my way through Julie's half of the Mars Bar we'd bought that morning, and then I looked over the top.

I couldn't believe my eyes. Marie Wood had gone all right, and Andrew.

But so had Julie. And so had George's bike. How on earth was I supposed to get down?

I sat there for ages, feeling a right chump. Not a car came past, not a policeman, not even a dog. I was cold and wet and miserable and hungry and just about to jump for my life, when Kevin came whistling down the posh part on his bike, his paper-bag swinging across his shoulder. Good old Kevin, all grin and freckles. I climbed down to him with as much dignity as I could muster in the circumstances.

'What's so funny?' I snapped.

He ignored me. 'Your papers are getting cold,' he said. 'Good job Julie saw me. She said you were in a bit of a fix.'

'What she walk off like that for?' I asked. 'She knew I'd never get down by myself. I'm glad I ate her bit of Mars Bar now.'

'She was trying to rescue Weird George's bike,' Kevin laughed. 'Marie Wood insisted that it must have been pinched, and she's taken it back to George's mum. You should have seen them, both hanging onto the bike and arguing their heads off all the way up the posh part, and old Andrew trailing behind them like a pet spider being taken for a walk!'

As we walked up the prom together I told Kevin about George and his carrier bags. Kevin's reaction was exactly the same as mine ... at first he thought George must be getting worse, to think of spending his school holidays doing that, and then he was intrigued with the possibility that it could work. We could get our baths back.

'Shall we help him, Kev?' I asked.

He swung himself up on his bike. 'We ought to talk about it first. D'you want to come over to our place tonight ... my mum and dad are going out to our Mike's. Bring Julie and George. See you!' And he was off.

I called for Julie after I'd done my paper-round, but she wouldn't come to George's house with me. I'd never been before. It was difficult to believe that two houses standing side by side could be so different from each other. Julie's was like a jumble sale, even when they'd made an effort. It was like a drawer that you had to remember not to open in front of visitors. But when George's mum opened up their door to me, I felt as if I ought to take my shoes off. They had a carpet – in the kitchen! And it looked brand new, throbbing with colours. It would have given my mum a head-ache, that carpet.

Even though Mrs Nightingale was getting tea ready there was nothing lying round the table or the work-tops, giving the game away. There was only Mr Night-ingale by the sink (my dad called him Florence), cutting potatoes into chips. He had them all laid out in a neat

18

row on the draining-board, identical, like soldiers.

'Well, love?' Mrs Nightingale's face crinkled politely.

'I've come to see George.' I nearly let the 'weird' out. My tummy clenched up inside me as I tried to swallow a giggle.

'George?' repeated Mrs Nightingale, as if she'd never heard of him. 'What do you want to see him for?'

'We were wondering if he'd like to come over to Kevin's for a bit, that's all.'

'To Kevin's, love? Our George?'

I was beginning to feel uncomfortable. I wished she'd ask me in, instead of leaving me out there in the draughty passage, with Julie standing at one end of it not daring to come any nearer in case she giggled. Mrs Nightingale obviously didn't know what to do with visitors. No wonder she kept her carpet so clean.

Her eyes clouded and unclouded as she tried to decide whether I was to be taken seriously or not. But Florence answered for her. 'The boy is sick,' he announced, not looking away from his chips. 'With a bad cold, being soaked to the skin every day, and a twisted ankle. The boy is in bed, sneezing, and waiting for his tea ...'

'Which you'd better get on,' his wife interrupted him. 'And remember the newspaper if you must have them greasy things.' She smiled at me as Florence busied himself sellotaping newspaper onto the tiled walls round the cooker.

I smiled back, amazed. 'How did he hurt himself, Mrs Nightingale?' I didn't want to go now, they were worse than George, these two.

'The boy claims he fell off a wall.' Florence spoke through sellotaped teeth. 'But what he was doing on the wall, I failed to ascertain. He ought to have more sense,' he sighed, spitting into the sink. 'But he hasn't.'

'He'd like to spend an evening with his friends, though,' Mrs Nightingale coaxed. 'He spends too much time on his own. Him and that blessed toytoyse.'

Julie choked at the other end of the passage.

Florence, with the flourish of a practising magician, whipped a gleaming chip-pan from the cupboard under the sink, and lit the gas. His wife watched anxiously as he jiggled the basket round in the fat.

'Can he come?' I asked.

'If the boy eats his chips, every one of them, and drinks up his tea, and two of you come for him in thirty minutes precisely' – he said this slowly, looking at his watch – 'and help him over the the road, and bring him back after an hour, it being time he has an early night and puts an end to coughs and sneezes, then yes, I'll say he can go.' He nodded at me courteously.

'Just you keep your eyes on that fat!' his wife muttered, smiling at me. 'And wipe that cooker if it spits!'

I backed off down the passage. Julie was beaming at me as if she'd given me a present.

'Spit, spit, spit,' Florence sang, through the open window. 'Spatter, spatter, spot!'

When Kevin and I went over for George in Thirty Minutes Precisely he was standing on one leg in the passage waiting for us. The kitchen door was closed. His ankle was bandaged up and his nose was running, but he looked cheerful enough. We hopped him across to Kevin's kitchen and balanced him on the rocking chair.

'I'm worried about my toytoyse,' he said. 'He was in my pocket when I fell off the baths' wall.'

'Oh, George, you haven't broken him, have you?' I asked. I felt awful about forgetting about him.

'No, but I gave him an awful shock. He's never looked out of his shell since.' He fished it out of his pocket. 'Look at him! I've never known him so quiet. You don't think he's had a heart attack, do you?'

Kevin picked it up thoughtfully and listened to the shell. 'Can't hear a thing. Are you sure it's still in there?'

George snatched it off him, panic-stricken. 'What d'you mean – where could he go without his shell?'

Kevin looked solemn. 'He could have wandered off and left it behind. I don't want to worry you, George, but our Mike knew someone who had a tortoise in their back yard. It never moved for six weeks. They thought it had hibernated, but it was in the summer holidays, you know. So when our Mike went round, he picked the shell up. And underneath it was full of maggots! And they all went running off round the garden!'

George clutched his tortoise to him in horror.

'Toytoyse, are you still in there?' he whispered down one of the ends. 'Toytoyse!'

Julie gave Kevin one of her acid looks. 'I thought you brought us here for a serious meeting, Kevin Proctor. Your tortoise will be all right, George, if you keep him warm. Put him back in your pocket and leave him alone.'

'It's my baths I'm most bothered about,' George moaned. 'If I have to leave it till my ankle gets better it'll never get done. We'll be back to school and the summer will be over and there'll be no point in the council opening them up and then it'll stand all winter and the gales will come and all the sand will pile up in it again and I'll have to start all over again.' He wiped his nose on his sleeve.

'Would you like us to help you with it, George?' said Kevin. 'I mean, I'm sorry about your tortoise, I really am, and I hope you didn't think we left you behind on purpose today. But we think it's a good idea, about the baths.'

'Do you?' George had perked up.

'We'll all help,' said Julie.

'Starting tomorrow,' I promised.

'And we'll find a safer way of getting in than you did,' finished Kevin, 'so there'll be no more accidents!'

'Hurray!' shouted George.

'Cooee!'

We all turned round to see Marie Wood's face pressed to the window. We stood up at once.

'Meeting closed,' said Kevin, opening the door.

'What's going on here, then?' sniffed Marie. She eyed the jug of lemonade on the table. 'Having fun?'

'We were, but we're going home now,' said Julie. 'We've got to get George back.'

We hopped him past her. There are times when I just can't be bothered with Marie. She's an odd kid – always has been. I mean, for instance, when we were in the Juniors, all the girls had to knit a red bonnet, the same shape as a baby's but child-sized. And Marie Wood actually *wore* hers! Her hair stuck out of all the holes where she'd dropped stitches, but she thought it was wonderful. 'I made this,' she kept telling everyone. As if they didn't know!

So you can see, what with that and her nosiness, we all felt quite sure we'd get on a lot better without her at clearing out the baths. None of us let on what we were doing, and next morning when we set off with our assortment of bags and buckets and saw her coming out of her front door we all shot down our side entry and hid till she'd gone past, and then raced down to the prom as if the wind was after us.

We'd noticed that part of the old jetty where Donkey-man Mooney used to tie up his donkeys had rotted away, and with a bit of heaving we managed to drag away a piece that was long enough to prop up against the back of the baths as a ladder. It was just about strong enough to take our weight. And we spent all day at it, scooping and scooping, getting wetter and tireder and more and more hungry and not one of us daring to be the first to say, 'Let's give up.' We'd been so eager to get started, but now it just didn't seem worth it.

'What are we wasting our time here for?' said Kevin. 'I don't even like swimming all that much.'

'What about George, then?' snapped Julie. 'He can't even swim!'

That was the sort of mood we were in, scratchy as cats, when we heard the familiar call.

'Cooee!'

'Marie Wood!' We all groaned.

'We know you're in there!' she shouted. 'We've come to help!'

I risked my head over the top of the parapet, and there she was, grinning up at me, dressed in her dad's boiler suit and a pair of yellow Wellies. Behind her was Andrew, a couple of beach buckets in one hand and a clutch of plastic spades in the other.

'What d'you want?' I sighed.

'Swimming pool campaign! We've come to help, haven't we, Andrew? Well, school holidays are such a bore!'

'How did she know about it?' growled Kevin.

'George told me, of course!' Her voice floated up to him. 'I went round this morning to play hop-scotch with him. ... Well, there's nothing else he *can* play, is there, with a poorly ankle like that. ... And I asked him how he'd hurt himself ... and he told me all about it.'

'We don't need any help, thank you,' said Julie firmly.

Marie ignored her. She found our jetty ladder and struggled up it, while we watched her helplessly. Fall off! I kept saying under my breath. I even considered tipping the ladder backwards so that she and Andrew would hurtle back down into the squelching bladder-wrack.

We waited for her sarcasm as she stood looking down at the soggy mess the pool was in. But her eyes sparkled with the challenge of it.

'Great, this,' she said. 'You've done great!'

'We haven't, Marie,' Julie began. 'It's hard work. We're worn out.'

'No wonder, if you've been at it all day. Have you?' And she gave us a concerned look, like my mum does sometimes if I don't want my tea.

She makes me laugh. 'Well, we haven't been sitting eating our sandwiches for the last five hours,' I snapped.

She prowled round the edge of the pool, like a house-buyer looking for faults. 'You kids have got the right idea, but you've got no sense of organisation,' she sighed. 'You must utilize your forces! It'll take us three days to clear out this lot, if you use my method.'

'What's that – a great big vacuum cleaner?' I was thinking of her mouth. It annoyed me to see that Kevin was actually interested.

'First,' she said. 'Don't work more than two hours at a time, or you get too bored and tired to do it properly. Am I right?'

Kevin nodded. I could have kicked him.

'And we work in teams throughout the day. Two hours on, four hours off, plenty of rest and time to work on the other things. We might as well get started now.'

'Well, I'm not,' I said. 'I'm going home for my tea.'

'Oh, you go, you go,' she said airily. 'Andrew and I can't wait to get started, can we, Andrew—'

'What about the rota, then?' Andrew asked. 'I'll be Julie's partner, if you like.'

Julie blushed and squinted across at me for help, but Marie wasn't having any of that nonsense.

'We'll start all that business tomorrow,' she said, already digging. 'And you needn't think you're going to spend all of your time chatting up Julie Mills, either. We'll have a proper rota. The two with the most fillings in their teeth start first. Next day we'll go in order of shoe sizes, and then oh, I don't know. Freckles, perhaps.' She looked up, her eyes shining. 'Won't it be great, having something to *do*, at last!'

'What about these other things you were talking about, Marie?'

That was Julie. Even she was getting interested now. Perhaps she actually wanted to be on the same shift as Andrew.

Trickles of mud ran down Marie's sleeve as she brushed her hair from her eyes. Cobs of it clung to her fringe.

'The parade!' she said. 'We have to be ready by Saturday!'

Parade?

'Heck, do I have to think of everything?' she said crossly. 'What's the point of doing all this work if nobody knows about it? What were you going to do, clear it out and then leave it to fill up with sand again?'

'Well, we hadn't exactly thought . . . '

'You're a waste of time, you lot!' She was digging with such venom now that spatters of mud like runny boils oozed down her face. 'We want to blaze the news across the town! We'll have a parade, with banners and music, we'll march through the market place in the middle of the morning when everyone's there, we'll get every kid in the town lined up behind us, and we'll drag the Lord Mayor down to see what we've done. We'll wake the town up, you'll see.'

She'd got us. And she knew it.

'And,' she added, waving her little blue plastic spade at us, 'we'll get them to put the roof on before the summer finishes.'

'Roof!' We all shouted at once. 'What roof?'

She sank back on her heels, right back in the mud, so it squeezed into the top of her Wellies and bubbled up against her thighs. Her mum's going to be mad with her, I thought briefly, but the pitying look in her eyes made me realise that her mind was on much higher things than clothes or mothers.

'The trouble with you kids is you've no vision,' she said softly. 'I'm not breaking my back just to persuade the council to put a bit of water in here and wait for six days of sunshine to warm it up. Oh no. I'm not that daft. I'm asking for an all-weather pool, with a convertible roof. That's what we're asking for.'

'Are we?' said Kevin.

Marie's legs sucked out of the mud as she stood up. 'We're asking them to notice the kids of this town for once! We want proper facilities! We want a real sports centre! We want the cafe open all the year round and ping-pong tables and a skittle-alley. We want to be able to swim winter and summer, hot days and cold. We want somewhere to go. What is there for kids in this town? You tell me! You tell me!' Her voice had risen to shouting pitch, matching the shriek of the gulls over our heads, but we were lost in silence. She was absolutely right. Suddenly I knew my mum was right about her, and that she was a born leader. She'd be someone important one day. A headmistress, or a lady mayoress. Maybe even a prime minister. Suddenly I liked her as much as I used to like her last year, when she had a pet monkey and we used to take it for walks.

There was nothing any of us wanted to do more now than to get to work on the swimming pool campaign.

'Right,' she said, squelching back comfortably onto her knees. 'That's settled.'

She only just managed to swallow the note of triumph in her voice, but none of us minded. The rain gathered together again and splattered in huge blobs around us, and we sat down with Marie in a cold damp circle and made our plans. No adults were to know about our campaign. They'd soon put a stop to it, if they knew we were climbing over walls and getting wet all day and trespassing. But every child under sixteen had to know by Saturday; they had to sign a petition, and they had to be ready to join in the march. And every single one of them had to be sworn to secrecy. The Swimming Pool Campaign was on.

Looking back, those were the best three days of that year. We all worked desperately hard when it was our turn to be on shift, trying to see who could fill the most bags. Marie and George won by miles, probably because they didn't talk to each other the whole time. Poor old George didn't know what had hit him when he came hopping down to the baths next day and was told to open his mouth and have his fillings counted first. We all pinched an old sheet each out of our airing cupboards and tore them into strips to make banners.

'Keep our pool open!'

'Let's splash again!'

'We oughta have water!'

Andrew and Kevin toured all the houses and got signatures from all the kids, telling them to be at the baths for a meeting on Saturday. That was all they knew, but when we passed any of them they would tap their nose and say 'S.P.C. 10', which meant that they had joined the swimming pool campaign and would be at the baths at ten on Saturday.

By Friday evening the pool was completely cleared. Andrew and Julie, the last two on shift, had swept up the whole of the sunbathing area and Kevin had pinched some paint from his dad's shed and touched up the stones round the fountain. George and Marie had painted a mural of seagulls against the far wall. It looked lovely, even in that grey light.

'All we need now is water,' sighed Julie.

'And sunshine,' I added.

'Or a roof!' Marie reminded me.

Our banners were rolled up neatly by the wall, with a drum and bugle that Andrew had borrowed from the scouts. Kevin played the only tune he knew on his mouth organ, and we all danced round, faster and faster, on the floor of the pool, kicking our feet like tap-dancers and shouting as the echoes cracked like pistol shots round the walls. We didn't want to go home, any of us. Perhaps we'd never be as close as this again.

We strolled back up to our street and sat on Julie's step, gossiping, till our mums called us in for our teas.

'You're spending a lot of time with that Marie Wood these days,' Mum said.

'Marie! She's great!' I said.

Mum smiled and went back to her book, and I smiled too.

Sometimes it was nice, having secrets from grown-ups.

*　　*　　*

Next morning I charged round with my papers, joyfully shouting S.P.C. 10 to every kid I came across, and then I cycled back up the entry to our house. Bacon sandwiches on a Saturday, always.

Mum was reading the *Local Advertiser* which Kevin had delivered, and hardly looked up when I came in. 'I see they've started on that swimming pool,' she said.

I grinned to myself. She wasn't getting anything out of me, if that was what she was after.

'Daft day though, Saturday, for council workers,' my dad said.

I started at him, a sudden clutch of dread inside me. 'Council workers?'

'Knocking it down. Starting today, it says here.'

Suddenly I heard Kevin's voice out in the street shouting 'The pool!' and saw Julie racing out of her entry. I saw George with Florence chasing after him, his pyjama top on still instead of a shirt, and I saw Andrew hurtling down the street banging on every window as he went past.

'S.P.C.!' he shouted, banging on mine. 'S.P.C. now!'

My mum beat me to the door.

'Tell me,' she said, leaning against it, her arms folded. 'What's it all about?'

'Let me go, Mum!' I shouted. 'I've got to go!'

'Muddy socks. Clothes soaked. Out all hours. I've been patient long enough, Bee Horton. I want to know what it's about.'

The tears were streaming down my cheeks as I told her about our wonderful secret, the hours and hours of work, the banners, the petition, the march.

30

'And now they're knocking it down! Without even asking us! Without even telling us, Mum! They don't care about us kids. Nobody cares.'

Mum looked at me, and then at Dad, and opened the door.

'You get down there, Bee,' she said. 'I'll be with you in a couple of minutes.'

I raced down the street. There were kids everywhere, following me, and more and more gathering the nearer I got to the baths. Marie was at the front shouting and shouting, her back pressed against the wall of the baths as though she was going to protect it with her life. She was shouting her head off but you couldn't hear a word she said because everybody else was shouting too. And drowning out everything was a crane, mounted and throbbing on the pavement like a huge beast waiting to be unleashed, roaring angrily as its driver revved the engine again and again in his impatience to get on with the job. Attached to it, and already swinging dangerously low, was the massive weight. When this was crashed against the baths' wall it would bring it crumbling down like a child's toy into the sand. One of the workmen climbed out of the cab and began moving the children out of the way, and sulkily, at last, Marie moved too, her mouth still working and no real words coming out at all.

I went over and stood with her and the rest of the committee, watching the man saunter back to his cab and climb in, and the machine move slowly forward. Another crane was drawing up now. It was only a matter of time now, before the building was brought down.

'How d'you get into this place?'

It was my mum, suddenly behind us. She made us all jump.

'We've got a ladder round the back,' said Kevin.

'Right. You get off round there,' Mum said. 'I'm going to try and stop this bloke for a minute. Then it's your turn. But you big ones' – she nodded to Kevin and Andrew – 'see no-one gets hurt. Right!'

Marie and the others streaked round the back of the baths. I stayed just long enough to watch my mum push her way through to the cab and hold something up to the driver. It was a packet of cigarettes. I've never seen my mum with a cigarette in her hand, before or since. She actually stuck one in the corner of her mouth. The two blokes in the cab both took one and when they handed the packet back Mum shouted something up to them. The driver switched off the engine, felt in his pockets, and leaned out of the cab to light her cigarette for her.

'Quick,' I yelled to the kids. 'Round the back. Quick!' And as the driver started up the cab Marie arrived, breathless and jubilant, on the top balcony. She was in! We'd taken over the baths! Like the tide turning the kids swarmed in a rush round the back of the baths, and I was nearly swallowed up in the stream of them. Andrew was holding the ladder at the bottom, letting one child at a time up it, and Kevin was at the top, helping them over the last bit. It seemed endless, but at last I was up, racing across the top balcony to stand with the others and look down at the row of silent adults with upturned faces who were gathering there to gape at us.

'Just you get down!' the crane-driver shouted, and

'Not till the Mayor arrives!' Marie shouted back.

We sent up a cheer that drove hundreds of gulls up into the sky.

Adults were arriving on the prom as fast as children appeared on the balcony. Cars began coming down with worried mums jumping out and shouting up to their kids. Constable Harvey strolled up, grinning, and stood back with his arms folded, watching the fun. Even the reporter from the *Local Advertiser* came tearing up with his camera. My mum was nowhere to be seen.

George banged the drum and hooted down the bugle and Kevin played his tune on his mouth-organ, and as the banners were found and passed up to the front we hoisted them up high and waved them like raggedy flags over our heads.

'Save our pool! Save our pool!' we chanted, louder and louder and faster and faster, and it was as if we couldn't stop, and there was some animal in us forcing us to do it. 'Save our pool! Save our pool!' the animal chanted.

It was then that the Lord Mayor arrived. Nobody had noticed him coming because he was only a little man anyway and he'd had to walk all the way down the posh part because all the roads were blocked up with people and cars. He held up his hands and we lowered our banners and silence fell.

The little man cupped his hands to his mouth.

'What you are doing is very dangerous and very naughty and you must come down at once. ...'

George cracked the drum and we all started singing again. We weren't going to be spoken to like that! He kept trying to say more things but we kept our chanting up, and he paced up and down waving to us to stop. Even the crane-drivers were grinning. The ice-cream man, finding his daily run along the prom halted, climbed out of his cab with a handful of ice-cream cones trying to tempt us down, and when none of us moved he handed them round to the adults. Everyone was laughing. The fierce little animal that had sparked us all off jeering and chanting in spite of ourselves seemed to simmer away and all of a sudden we were enjoying ourselves, singing one song after another while our mums and dads chatted and laughed below us. And then a kind of miracle happened.

I turned to Kevin. 'Have you noticed?' I said. 'The sun's shining!'

The rain had stopped for the first time for days and days and days. The clouds were drifting out with the tide and underneath like a brand new carpet that had been hidden under layers of dust the sky was as blue as I'd ever seen it. The old sun stretched itself like a cat.

I saw that the Mayor had been joined by a group of people, including my mum and Mr Spud Murphy, our headmaster from school, and that one of them had a key. As they came towards the baths' door and started to open it the singing voices stopped one by one and staggered into silence. The little animal was stirring again – I could feel it. Any minute now, I thought, the grown-ups would be in here and those kids at the front will be roaring down the steps to drive them out. 'It's your turn,' my mum had said. Is that what she would have wanted us to do?

'Don't move, anyone,' I shouted. 'Just keep still.' Like lightning my order was passed round.

Now we all turned away from the street and looked down into the inside of the pool; and, as the mayor and his officials and all those other people with my mum walked through the door and into the central area that we had cleaned out, it was as if they were actors on a stage, and we, high up on the balcony on all four sides, were the audience.

And that was how we came to hear every word that was said.

'Haven't they done well! Doesn't it look great!'

'A lot better than the last time I saw it – '

'They must have worked hard, them kids – '

Their voices buzzed backwards and forwards like surprised bluebottles.

'And there were only six of them, you know.' That was my mum. She looked proud.

'But they've all signed. Every kid in the place has signed. Who'd have thought they'd want to keep this place going?'

'Why not? There's nowhere else for them, is there?'

They'd all been pacing round the big square of the pool, and at this last remark they stood round and faced Mr Murphy. He bent down towards the little Lord Mayor.

'What a pity the building wasn't put up for sale, sir,' he said.

'For sale? This place? Who'd want to buy this place?'

'We would, sir.' said Mr Murphy. 'The community.'

Not a breath. We all looked at each other, not daring to speak.

'Community?' Julie mouthed at me. But I nodded. I'd heard my mum going on about it often enough. The community meant everyone who lived in a place, and Mum was on some committee that met every month and, according to her, talked a lot and did nothing. She was chuntering away to Mr Murphy now, all right. I could see she was trying to talk him into something. At last he spoke up.

'We're all concerned about the fact that there's nothing for our children to do round here,' he said to the Mayor. 'We were trying to raise money for a youth club. There's a little factory coming up for sale – '

'But perhaps we could put the money to better use here,' one of the parents said. 'If this is what the children want.'

'And we'd get something out of it then,' another parent put it. 'I've always liked this place myself.'

They were all chipping in now, while the little Mayor stood in the middle of them, his mouth opening and shutting and his fluttery hands jumping in and out of his pockets as he tried to butt in. 'But . . . '

We were hanging on to every word that was spoken. I breathed a reminding shush to everyone round me. One false move – one little squeak from the jeering animal in us that people like the Mayor so detested, and all would be lost.

'What are you saying, Mr Murphy?' said the Mayor. He suddenly seemed rather exhausted, a fidgety little man who was wanting his dinner. He glanced up at us

36

as if he'd forgotten all about us and was annoyed to find us eavesdropping. No-one moved.

'We wonder if you would care to reconsider your plan to demolish the baths' – Mr Murphy nodded round at the other members of his committee gathered round him – 'and put it up for sale. I think we'd be interested in making an offer for it.'

Marie couldn't contain herself any longer. 'Hurray for Mr Murphy!' she shouted, and, 'Three cheers for Spud!' Like cannon balls the cheers were sent up from the balconies.

We'd won; we knew it. We set up our singing again, but very gently, as the Mayor moved out and his officials followed him. Mr Murphy and my mum and all the other members of the community group that she'd dragged away from their morning cups of coffee and visits to the hairdressers filed after him. We all piled down the steps and across the sunbathing area into the crowd on the prom. We followed the Mayor's group as they walked up the posh part to their cars, and we raised our banners and banged our drum and blew our bugle and sang our heads off, through the market and down the main street to the steps of the town hall.

'I can't believe it,' I said to Julie, as we sat there with out arms held out and our faces turned up to the sun to get brown. 'The end of the Campaign!'

'That's what you think,' Marie said. 'We've got the money to raise next. Our work's only just started. Just you wait and see.'

How right she was.

2. Fingers Finnigan and the Saturday Matinee

Saturday morning, every week till we were about twelve, we used to go to the matinee at the picture house on the prom. It was great. When the wind was blowing in really strong from the sea you could taste the grit of sand in your interval ice-cream, and when it rained, of course, you avoided the back seats or you got dripped on. We always saw the same films five or six times in a year, so it didn't matter that the projector broke down so often; in fact, we looked forward to it happening. The film would suddenly flicker and jump about, and the voices would come in at the wrong speed, and then the screen would go blank. We'd all set up a howl of disappointment, and then we'd start jeering and whistling and stamping our feet and banging crisp-bags, and Mr Oliver the manager would come running down the aisle shouting at us:

'You can clear out, the lot of you! Noisy little brats. I'm not having this racket, do you hear me? I'll knock your teeth in!' We'd jeer all the louder at this, knowing that he wouldn't turn us out because we'd paid for our seats, and also knowing that there was more fun to follow.

On his rapid way down the aisle Mr Oliver would suddenly yank one of the smaller kids out of its seat and plonk it on the stage in front of the screen, where it would stand squirming about and scratching itself while he tried to shut the rest of us up.

'Be quiet now, be quiet the lot of you. You're worse than a load of monkeys. If you'll all shut up, we're about to have our very own talent show!' He'd press his hands forward as if he was squashing the noise back, and his voice would squeeze through our din like a siren pushing through fog. 'And here is our first brave contestant. Come on you lot, or I'll learn you some manners. Three cheers for our first contestant!'

And we'd stand on our seats cheering the house down while Mr Oliver clung on to the kid so that it didn't run back to its place, and when he eventually shut us up again the first contestant would always have thought of something; a song or a tap-dance or a joke, because it would have seen the bar of chocolate in Mr Oliver's hand. Anyway, even to perform badly on stage would have been better than to suffer the enraged disappointment and cat-calls of the audience if you went back to your seat without doing anything.

After the first contestant had received its chocolate bar and we'd all roared our applause there was no end to the queue of performers, and no end to Mr Oliver's supply of chocolates, and it was all he could do to shut us up again and get us to settle down and watch the film

when it was mended.

We were petrified, though, in case any of us got picked. ... Julie devised a little sketch so that we'd be prepared, at least. She persuaded Kevin to be in it because he never minded making a fool of himself. We practised it in the entry every night for a week, with audiences of cats and pigeons and several people leaning out of their bedroom windows. It was quite good, especially Kevin's ballet dance; by the time Saturday came round again we knew without doubt that it was better than anything anyone had ever done at the picture-house – maybe better even than any of the films we'd ever seen. We sat through the film that day not watching any of it because we were so nervous. Julie went to the toilet three times. But the projector didn't break down. We marched up to Mr Oliver as he was waiting to see us all out.

'Tell him!' Julie hissed to Kevin.

'Mr Oliver, can we do our show? We've been practising it all week. Please, Mr Oliver.'

He looked down at us in annoyance. 'I've had enough of you kids to last me six months. Clear off, you little pests.'

'It's dead good – it's brilliant.'

'So's Tarzan, and I don't want to see that again today neither. Scram.'

We ran off, relieved really that we weren't going to have to do our act, but mad at Mr Oliver for turning us down.

'I'm not going there again!' panted Julie. 'Are you, Kev? Are you, Bee?'

'No, I'm not, it's sissy.' said Kevin. 'It's full of little kids. I'd rather be doing football practice with our Mike.'

'And his films are rotten lousy, anyway,' I said.

But we all felt a bit guilty saying that, because we knew that the Saturday matinee was great. Anyway, the pictures were out, and the ice-cream parlour was in, and we settled down to our new routine as if we'd been doing it for years.

Then one day Julie's mum asked her to take her little brother Robert to the Saturday matinee. He'd been helping her to make cakes for the swimming pool fund, and as he hadn't eaten any of them she reckoned he deserved a treat.

'But Mum, I never go there. I haven't been there for years.'

'Well, you can go today.'

'I'm going to the ice-cream parlour with Bee.'

'Go to the matinee with her instead.'

'She wouldn't be seen dead at the matinee, Mum. Only the little kids go there.'

'Julie Mills, if I have to tell you once more you'll be up them stairs two at a time. You're taking our Robert to the pictures and that's flat!' She dropped the pile of nappies she'd been sorting and pushed Julie and Robert out into the street, and slammed the door on them.

I was just about to call for Julie to come up to the shops with me. I had my new sweater on, and I was amazed to see she wasn't wearing her new skirt. We always wore our newest clothes on a Saturday morning.

'I can't come with you, Bee,' she said, and she had the end of the world in her voice. 'I've got to take our Robert to the pictures.'

'Pictures? Not the Saturday matinee? You poor old thing.'

We walked along in silence the three of us, Robert's excitement at going to the pictures for the very first time completely squashed by our depression. When we arrived at the picture house, with all that screaming mass of little kids writhing and kicking in the queue outside I knew that I couldn't go in. Not even for Julie.

'I'll see you, Julie,' I said. 'I think I'll call for Di.' That was a mean touch and I felt a gloating kind of cruelty when I said it. Di was Julie's friend really, from the convent school.

'Wait, Bee!' said Julie in anguish. 'I'm coming with you.'

Robert's face began to pucker.

'Do you really want to see this film, our Robert?' Julie asked him. He nodded, too distressed to speak.

'Right. Now when these doors open, you run in, and you chuck your money at the man sitting in the little box. Just follow the other boys and girls, you'll be all right. And I'll see you out here at twelve o'clock. You mustn't go home on your own. Promise. Cross your heart and hope to die. Have a nice time.'

We dashed off before he could protest, and spent the rest of the morning in Di's house, listening to her records. But I can't say we enjoyed it, either of us. All her records were about fifty years old, anyway, and we kept thinking of Robert's stricken little face, and the size of him, with all those screaming kids round him. 'My mum'll kill me,' Julie kept saying.

Once he was inside the picture house and the audience had settled itself into some kind of order to watch the film Robert quite enjoyed himself. He still wasn't quite sure what to do, but he decided that as long as he sat there till the clock in the corner pointed to twelve there was nothing to worry about. He noticed that the boys sitting in the same row as him all sat on the tops of their seats with their legs over the backs of the seats in front, and Robert tried to do the same, but his seat kept banging down so that he thumped his neck on the seat back, and eventually the usherette came down and slapped his legs for him and threatened to turn him out. He sat very still, even though he could only see half the screen when he sat on the seat properly. He couldn't really hear now because everyone was getting noisy, but if he craned his neck round he could see the clock. That gave him some sort of comfort.

Then the dreadful thing happened. The film flickered wildly, the voices of the cowboys slurred to a drunken drawl, and then into silence. Immediately everyone in the cinema sent up a howl, then started booing and hissing and stamping their feet and thumping each other. Robert started up in terror. A man came down from the back, waving his fists and shouting at everyone to shut up, and before Robert knew what was happening he'd been scooped up under the man's arm, with his head sticking out one way and his legs sticking out the other, and he'd been plonked on the middle of the stage facing a mass of open mouths and waving arms and a cheer that threatened to force the roof off.

'Don't you worry, titch,' the man whispered down his ear. 'Sing them a little song and you'll get this bar of chocolate and everyone will be happy. See?'

But Robert didn't see. The man held out his arms and the cheering stopped like a cloud closing out sunlight. Everyone was watching him, and all he knew was that he couldn't remember one single song and that he wanted to go home. The silence suffocated him. He suddenly broke away from Mr Oliver and ran down the steps at the end of the stage. Kids sent up their jeering and laughing and whistling again and stuck legs out to trip him up as he ran down the aisle, past his seat, panicked when he couldn't find it, and charged through the doors at the back. He pushed another door that could have opened out into the street but mercifully didn't, as it was too early to meet Julie, and he clanked in the darkness through an armoury of brushes and mops till he sank down, safe at last, in a spidery corner. He curled up there, hiccuping softly, going over and over again the snatches of songs that he could remember, until at last he stuck his thumb in his mouth, closed his eyes, and went to sleep.

When Julie and I arrived at the picture house just after twelve there wasn't a child in sight. Mr Oliver was locking the front doors, and chewing away at a bar of nutty chocolate. Julie asked him if he'd seen a little boy, and he said he'd seen so many little boys that morning that he never wanted to see another one again in his life, and he gave us both a packet of chewing-gum from his pocket before driving off to watch the football. We sat on the steps, forlornly popping our gum and not knowing what on earth to do next.

'I daren't go home without him, Bee. Mum'll kill me.' Julie moaned. 'And if he's got home already without me, she'll still kill me. I daren't go home. Ever.'

I pulled her up. 'We'll have to go back,' I coaxed her. 'What if he gets lost on the way? You go down the prom, and I'll go up the main road way. One of us is bound to find him.'

But neither of us did. I met Julie again at the top of our street, and she was feeling sick, I could tell. I wasn't feeling much better myself. I remember I was chewing and chewing that rotten gum that Mr Oliver had given us, even though all the flavour had gone. Normally I'd

45

have spat it down a drain or stuck it under someone's window-sill, but it helps to calm your agitation, somehow, to keep chewing, especially if you slop it round so it makes a lot of noise.

'Now what do we do?' wailed Julie. 'He's been kidnapped, I know he has. Poor little Robert. He was quite nice, really.'

I told her to wait in the entry while I went and asked her mum if she was back home yet. Mrs Mills was bound to say, 'No she isn't, but our Robert is, and I'll skin her alive when she get back.'

If he was there.

But there was no answer when I knocked on the door. The house was quiet. I peered through the window. Mrs Mills was fast asleep, with a pile of folded washing beside her and her head on the table. The little ones would be upstairs having their nap, and she was obviously overwhelmed with the peace that having the room to herself offered. I dodged away and off down the entry to Julie, because any minute now my mum would be wondering about the shopping she'd sent me off for that morning. It was getting on for one o'clock. We sat and sat, and one by one Kevin and Marie and George slid out and joined us, and they all whistled in sympathy when we told them we'd lost Robert. And still we sat, chewing, and waiting for him to come home.

Robert was just about waking up then. As he stretched himself he kicked over a broom, and a mouse scuttled up to him and away again. A spider uncurled itself and loped across the floor, and everything was silent again.

46

Robert groped around in the blackness until he came to a door, and pushed it open into a colder blackness. He crawled across a cold tiled floor, and found a door that opened into a wider blackness that was colder still. He stood up, and his feet scuffed soft carpeting, and his reaching fingers touched the soft pile of fabric. He pressed down on a hard surface, and it flipped down away from his hand and back again with a thump that reminded him of that morning, and getting his legs slapped for sitting on the seat top. So that was what it was. He groped forward, and touched another seat-top, and on and on until the seat-tops finished and there was emptiness in front of him. He forced himself to run across it, and came up against the hard edge of the stage. That was all right, then. He knew where he was, and he knew what he had to do.

At just about the same time Fingers Finnigan was wriggling through a tiny back window that only he knew about, and which he'd been keeping an eye on for weeks. Now at last his patience was rewarded, and Mr Oliver had left it unhinged. Fingers had spent the last half hour pacing up and down the back yard of the picture house, watching the window like you watch a coin that's been dropped on the pavement. But he knew he'd no excuse now, no reason for putting it off any longer. His first real chance to do a real burglary. 'You've got to do it, boyo,' he told himself sternly, nibbling his thumbnail. 'You're the black sheep of the family. Two brothers and a dad serving time, and you've never even hopped off the bus without paying. Come on. Close your eyes, and jump!'

He coaxed his fingers under the window edge, and prised it up like a cockle-shell opening. Then he hauled himself up, closing his eyes because he had a dread of heights, and wriggled down into a steep drop that made his bones jump. All he had to do now was to find his way to the foyer. He'd seen Mr Oliver leaving that morning, wrestling with a key and a big chocolate bar, and nothing else in his hands at all. That meant that the morning's takings would still be there, chinking coins and rustling notes all warm and snug in a little box. He forced himself to grope his way through the dark quiet building, not daring to turn on his torch because he was more frightened of jumping shadows than he was of the dark. His heart leapt like a fish inside him. 'Keep still, you great fool,' he whispered to it. 'You're making more noise than a steam train. Keep going, Fingers old son. Just think what your old dad'll say when he comes back home from the nick. Fingers, I'm proud of you, he'll say! Think of that!' And he nosed his way along in a blackness that danced with policeman's eyes and boomed with policemen's voices.

Then he heard the voice. A tiny white voice in the darkness, spiralling round him like a web.

> 'Away in a manger
> No crib for a bed
> The little Lord Jesus
> Lay down his sweet head. . . .'

'Glory be,' moaned Fingers to himself. 'It's an angel. At a time like this. Wouldn't you know your luck, Fingers. An angel!'

48

The angel began again, and Fingers felt his throat tighten with the sweetness of it. Wasn't there more wonderfulness in the hearing of this than in the snatching up of a jangling old cash-box, he asked himself, and nodded gently. There was. There was. But what he wanted most of all was to see the angel. That would be a thing to tell his dad on visiting day. He marvelled that angels didn't light up of their own accord, but luckily he had his torch in his pocket. He pointed it in the direction of the voice and switched it on. He gazed in awe at the golden hair and creamy skin of the child in the light.

Robert stopped singing.

'Oh, go on, sir!' Fingers begged. 'Don't mind me. It was beautiful, sir.'

'Was it?' Robert was relieved. 'Can I have my chocolate now?'

Doubt crept into Fingers' mind, and danced away again. He knew where the chocolate kiosk would be, and as he turned to go into the foyer he heard the angel jump off the stage and scamper up the aisle after him. Again doubt like a butterfly bobbed across his mind. He shone his torch over the trays of chocolates, picked out the three that he liked best, and handed them to Robert.

'Don't you have to pay for them?' asked Robert, and his eyes in the torchlight searched solemnly for Fingers' own, and held them.

'Crikey,' Fingers thought, emptying out his pockets. 'This is a fine turn-up. Here am I all set to find meself a week's wages and I end up having to pay out for chocolate!'

As Robert's mouth closed round a good half of the

biggest bar, Fingers reflected sadly that this was probably no angel after all, but an ordinary little boy.

'Can I go home now?' asked Robert, his voice thick with chocolate, and it was then that Fingers knew for certain that his angel had flown away, and had left him in real trouble.

'Did you get locked in here, kid?' he asked hoarsely.

Robert nodded, chewing.

'Does anyone know you're here?' Fingers had to force his voice to keep down, though he felt like shouting with anxiety.

In the torchlight Robert's eyes swam with tears. 'Our Julie said I'd got to meet her outside at twelve o'clock. She'll be mad with me now.'

But Fingers was sitting with his head in his hands, moaning softly. The girl would be outside now, bound to be. She'd have her dad with her by now. They'd have found Mr Oliver, they'd have fetched the police, they'd break open the door. Nicked, and without even pinching anything. He'd be a laughing-stock.

He grabbed Robert's hand suddenly and jerked him over to the back of the cinema. He lifted him up to the window.

'Stick your head out, kid. Can you see anyone?'

'No!' Robert clasped the two bars of chocolate tightly. You never knew with grown-ups, they might be taken off him in exchange for his freedom.

'Right!' said Fingers. 'I'm going to shove you out, and you're going to fly like the wind before your dinner gets cold. But you haven't seen me, have you?'

'Haven't I?'

'No. You haven't seen me. I'm a secret.'

Robert sighed as he slid down to the ground. 'I know who you are, though.'

Sweat gathered like blisters on Fingers' forehead.

'Do you?'

'Course I do. You're my guardian angel, aren't you?'

Fingers heart rose inside him. He forced his eye to wink. 'Fancy you guessing,' he whispered. 'Now scram.'

We all charged into Robert just as he was running out of the back yard of the picture house. Mr Oliver was with us, still shouting at us because he was going to miss the kick-off.

'I told you!' he said triumphantly. 'He's been hiding from you, the little monkey. Wants a good hiding and locking up in a dark cupboard for a week.' You could tell from his face how relieved he was.

'I haven't been hiding. I've just climbed out of that window round the back.' Robert's voice was muffled because Julie was hugging him so tightly and also because his mouth was full of chocolate. I wondered if he'd pinched it.

'And if you've left it open I'll have every burglar in the county after my takings. And my chocolate. I don't know why I bother with kids, I really don't.' Mr Oliver hovered. He made a sudden lunge at Robert. I thought he was going to hit him at first, I really did, but he picked him up and squeezed him between his arms like a hot water bottle. 'Little chump,' he muttered. 'You poor little chump. It'll serve me right if I have been burgled, Titch.'

As he spoke I saw Robert's eyes flicker slightly, and I turned round to see what he was looking at. I could have sworn I saw something move very quickly across the yard, and over the wall on the other side. But it may have been the shadow of a cloud, or a gull flying very low. And it didn't matter. Robert was safe.

3. Mr Punch

Mr Punch used to stand just outside Woolie's every Saturday morning, smiling and smiling at all the children. His long nose and bristled chin came towards each other, as if they were trying to meet, but couldn't quite manage it because his mouth was smiling so much. He had red shiny cheeks that you felt you could peel off, like apple skins, and his hair was white and thick. I think he was the kindest man I knew. His pockets were always bulging with bags of sweets, and as you were going past he'd beckon you up to him and then hold out a handful of sweets to you. We used to go past him on purpose, three or four times, and always he'd smile and smile until you'd come right up to him, and drop a couple of sweets into your hand. I only ever saw him on a Saturday, and I never saw him come or go. He was just always there, like those little statues of blind children you see outside chemist's shops sometimes, holding collecting boxes; or the big cardboard cut-out of a chef with a menu chalked on his apron that they propped up outside the baths' cafe. Julie reckoned that Woolie's probably kept him in a stock-cupboard all week, and just brought him out on a Saturday.

Then Nicola Winkle, who lives across the entry from me, told me that he lived in the nursing-home on the prom where her auntie works as a cleaner, and that he was a millionaire.

'He's got enough money hidden in his cupboard to buy six roofs for that swimming pool, you know,' she said. 'I don't know why you're wasting your time collecting money from jumble sales. He could buy us a new roof tomorrow, but he's too mean.' Nicola Winkle tells terrible fibs – when she had a brace on her front teeth she told us it was a family heirloom and that her great-grandmother had been the first to wear it, and she also told us that she had such good legs that her mother wanted to insure then before she started playing hockey at the big school.

She was really mad when I said I didn't believe her about Mr Punch. 'Go and see for yourself, then,' she said crossly. 'He makes a right mess of his room too, my Auntie Rosemary says.'

She was talking to me over the top of their wall, but it was a bit high and she kept disappearing when her fingers got tired of holding on. 'He must have pots of money to afford all those sweets he gives out!' her voice said, and then her face came into view as she levered herself up again. 'Anyway, my Auntie Rosemary's *seen* all his money. He keeps it locked up in his cupboard but she caught him once, counting it. She heard him! She heard this paper rustling when she went in, and as soon as he saw her he pushed it back in the cupboard, quick. She says he's a messy devil and he's a mean old faggot, too.'

'He never is,' I said. She was going down again. I watched her fingers slipping on the wall and waited for her head to come back up. 'He's the kindest man I know.'

'My Auntie Rosemary says that even with all that money he's got, d'you know what he does? He *pinches* shoe boxes!'

'You're making it up, Nicola Winkle! What would he want to go pinching shoe boxes for?'

'To keep his money in, of course!' she sighed. 'He's got dozens of them in that cupboard of his, and they're all stuffed with money!'

She dropped off again, and didn't bother to come back up. 'He's batty, you know. He plays with plasticine, too. He's like a big kid!'

Kevin came out of his backyard with his bike. 'What's Twinkle-Knickers on about?' he asked me.

'Some daft tale about Mr Punch,' I giggled. 'She reckons he pinches shoe boxes to keep his millions in.'

'I can hear you, laughing at me,' came her voice from behind the wall.

'I'll tell you something else about him, too. Some of those sweets he doles out aren't sweets at all – they're plasticine lumps wrapped up in shiny paper. He's batty!'

On the Saturday of that week Julie and I were doing our mums' shopping, as we always did. We used to finish up at the ice-cream parlour opposite Woolie's after I'd collected my paper-round money. As we went past Woolie's Mr Punch was there, as usual, smiling and

smiling, bending down to the little ones as they came up to him for sweets. I told Julie about Nicola Winkle's story.

'He must be ever so lonely,' she said. 'No-one ever talks to him, have you noticed? I mean, they just grab his sweets and run off.'

'Shall we talk to him?' I said. 'Come on, let's go and say, something.'

'What can we say, though?' Julie's dead shy about talking to people. She wouldn't make a telephone call for anything, not even if her house was on fire.

'We'll think of something,' I said. As we went up to him he turned round to us, still smiling, holding out a bag of toffee whirls. They did look like plasticine, but I took a chance.

I asked him if he knew Nicola Winkle's Auntie Rosemary, but he just smiled and handed Julie a sweet.

'Your turn,' I mouthed at her.

'Is your name really Mr Punch?' she asked nervously. He laughed and shook his head. His lips parted slightly, and a strange gurgling sound came out.

'Pardon?'

He gurgled again, and she squinted over to me.

'Do you live on the prom?' I asked. He nodded. 'In the green nursing-home?'

He nodded again. 'Then Nicola Winkle's Auntie Rosemary cleans your room for you.'

He frowned, still smiling, and waved to a little boy who was watching out hopefully for the bag of sweets. 'Bye, Mr Punch,' I said, as we drifted away and over the road to the ice-cream parlour.

Nicola Winkle was already in there, watching us smugly. 'Told you he was batty, didn't I?'

'Course he's not batty. He can't talk properly, that's all. And he's mad on little kids. What's batty about that?' I really hated Nicola Winkle. I'd rather have Marie Wood than her any day, and that was saying something. But Mr Punch had intrigued me now. That evening I rushed my paper-round so I would be finished and outside Woolie's by five. Mr Punch was still there, nodding and smiling to the little ones, but as soon as the manager of Woolie's came out to lock the door he moved away, as if it was clocking-off time and his week's work was done. He wandered round the back of the shop through the goods entrance, where new stock is delivered and rubbish is chucked out in big skips waiting to be picked up by the bin men, and when he came back out he had a shoe-box tucked under each arm. He nodded and chuckled to me as he made his way off down to the prom, to the huge green house where all those old people lived, white faces at the windows, staring at the old brown tide as it rolled in each day and relentlessly crept away again. Was that how Mr Punch spent his days, I wondered, when he wasn't watching the busy Saturday shoppers and handing out sweets to the children? I didn't think about him again until the next week. I didn't have time, we seemed to be busy every day with different schemes to raise money for the new pool roof. But the next Saturday we were out doing our mums' shopping again. I was waiting for Julie to come out of the greengrocers' when I noticed a little crowd standing outside Woolie's, a woman shouting, and Constable

59

Harvey striding across the road. I yanked Julie out of her queue and we ran down the road to see what was happening. A little boy was crying, and his mother, Mrs Bean who does our school dinners, was shouting at poor Mr Punch. Women were arguing with her and with each other, and on the pavement was a spilt bag of boiled fruit sweets.

'What's up?' sighed Constable Harvey. He'd just dragged himself away from a traffic jam. You could still hear it honking away at the roundabout.

'That man!' said Mrs Bean, pointing at the bewildered Mr Punch, 'has just given my little boy a sweet!'

'And?' prompted Constable Harvey.

'But I've told Gary he must never take sweets from strangers. It shouldn't be allowed. It should be against the law, sergeant. I've heard things about him. You should move him on.'

'But he isn't a stranger,' interrupted Kevin, who'd been going past on his bike. 'That's Mr Punch! We've known him for years!'

Well. That started them all off, then. Nicola Winkle said she'd seen him pinching shoe boxes. Marie Wood's mum came down amazingly in his favour by saying she'd rather he spent his pension on sweets for kids than on beer like her father-in-law; another woman who must have been Nicola Winkle's Auntie Rosemary said he's enough pound notes to paper the town hall with, and that she wouldn't eat one of his sweets if he offered her one even, she knew what was in them. Mrs Bean said that wasn't the point, he'd no right to stand there making her child take sweets when she'd forbidden him to.

60

'He stares at children, that's what I don't like,' another woman put in. 'But he never says a word to them, have you noticed? I don't trust him one bit.'

All this was addressed to Constable Harvey, who had had one of Mr Punch's sweets every Saturday morning of his beat for years, but wouldn't let on, and who had half his mind on the traffic jam still.

'I'd better go and shift this lot,' he muttered. 'You carry on arguing among yourselves till I get back.'

As soon as the policeman had turned his back a young man in a studded leather jacket slid his foot forward to cover one of the sweets. He thought no-one had noticed him, but I kept my eye on his big brown boot. I knew he was going to keep it there till everyone had gone, and then eat the sweet underneath it. He looked round, whistling jauntily, with his hands stuck in his jacket pockets and his foot pointed in front of him like a booted ballet-dancer.

And then I turned to see that Mr Punch himself had slipped away. 'He's over there,' Julie whispered to me. 'Look'. And we just made him out, threading through the traffic jam, making off down the posh part to the nursing home on the prom.

The women stood round helplessly, their anger fizzling out like fireworks in the rain. 'Well,' said Mrs Wood. 'I hope you're satisfied, Mrs Bean.'

'I am!' Mrs Bean said. 'I am. He'd never have sneaked off like that if he hadn't got a guilty conscience.'

The young man in the leather jacket moved his other foot over a second sweet. He swayed backwards and forwards, lost his balance, and as he leaned back I heard

61

the scrunch of the sweet as his heavy boot crunched it for good. He sighed, disgusted with himself, and walked off.

Mrs Bean's Gary bent down to pick up another of the sweets on the pavement and she slapped his hand, making him cry again. The scattered sweets looked like fragments of broken glass, and I suddenly thought of a coloured glass vase that my mum had dropped once during an argument with my dad, and cried over because it had been a present from him.

'Poor Mr Punch!' Kevin said softly behind me. 'I bet he never comes here again.'

And he didn't. We looked for him as the Saturdays came and went but we never saw him outside Woolie's again. Nicola Winkle didn't know any more about what had happened to him than we did; her Auntie Rosemary had packed her job in, she said, because one of the old ladies at the nursing home had died and left her enough money to live on for the rest of her life, but I knew that was a fib because she'd got a job collecting money for the pools. I'd seen her doing it!

But we all felt bad about the way old Mr Punch had slipped away like that with everyone arguing about whether he had the right to be giving away sweets, and him not being able to talk well enough to defend himself. It was Kevin who suggested that we should go and visit him at the nursing home.

'What would we say, though?' asked Julie anxiously. 'We can't just go in and grin at him.'

And then I suggested we could take him some empty

shoe-boxes. At least it would be an excuse for going, even if it was a daft present.

None of us had ever been to the nursing home before. It was the biggest house on the prom, and had balconies in front of the windows. You sometimes saw old people sitting out on them, tucked into tartan blankets, but more often than not you just saw them through the glass, gazing out at the sea. I hated the place. I hated the colour of the paintwork, and as we walked up the sloped path to the front door, I hated the silence of it. The matron of the home bristled at the sight of three children on her quiet doorstep.

'I'm busy,' she said. 'If it's jumble you've come for, we've none today, thank you.'

'We've come to see Mr Punch,' I said.

'Who? Who? Never heard of him.'

'Well, at least he looks like Mr Punch,' I said helplessly. 'You know . . . his nose . . . and his chin. . . .'

'Yes . . .?' she looked interested.

'And we've brought him these. . . .' I held out the shoe-boxes.

'Oh, you mean Mr Deacon. Mr *Deacon*. Not Mr Punch. Dear dear, what a silly name.' She tittered in spite of herself. 'Mr Punch! I never thought of that. Why didn't you say so in the first place? If anyone could do with a visitor, that man could.'

'Isn't he well?'

'I don't know what he isn't, but he isn't the man he was. I've never seen such a change in anyone. Can't get a smile out of him, and he was the life and soul of the house! Spends all day in his room, moping, tidying up, and *that's* not him. I'd rather have him cheerful, and his room in a tip again any day.'

'Can we go and see him, though, just to take him these shoe-boxes?'

She sighed. 'I don't think he's got much use for shoe-boxes any more. After all these years. Come on, though, you might as well have five minutes with him, if he'll see you.'

She led us down a wide shiny corridor past several green doors, rapped sharply on one of them, and opened it quickly. Her voice changed into the coaxing tone old ladies use for three-year-olds. 'Now, Mr Deacon. Who's a lucky boy? Who's got *three* visitors all in one day?'

She pushed us in, and then pulled me back into the corridor. Her breath was thick, like my mum's sometimes when she's cooked us something she's pleased with. She pressed a key into my hand, and whispered right into my ear, 'You might just perk him up. If he starts looking chirpy, give him this key. Right!' I nodded, like a conspirator, sliding the key into the pocket of my jeans. 'I'll just pop off and do the temperatures; leave him to you.'

Mr Punch sat with his back to us, staring out of the window. But his room didn't look out across the sea. It was at the back of the house, and gave out onto the flat roof of the kitchen, the little yard with tufts of grass sprouting in the sandy soil, and the high red brick wall that closed everything in.

'Hello, Mr Deacon,' Kevin said. He didn't answer, didn't even turn his head round, or move.

I went over to him, not quite knowing what to do. I sat on the edge of the bed, and looked round the room. There wasn't a thing out to show any trace of possession: not a book, or a picture, or a piece of clothing, even. All the room contained was the bed, the table and chair, and a cupboard.

I put the two shoe-boxes on the table in front of him. 'We thought you might need these.'

He tossed the lids off the boxes and smoothed down the crinkled tissue paper inside them. He looked at me, then at Kevin and Julie. He nodded towards the bed, and they both sat down on it. The silence in that little room reminded me of my grandad's house – it seemed to soak into the walls and the furniture, as if there was so much of it that however much noise you made it couldn't make any lasting impression. The silence would eat it up and take over again. Kevin plucked at the frayed bit on his jeans. Julie cleared her throat so suddenly that Mr Punch jumped, and that started her giggling silently; she always does when she's on edge. I could feel the bed shaking as she tried to control herself.

'We've all missed you,' I said, in case he'd noticed her. 'I think all the children are missing you.'

He nodded and cocked his head, taking me in. I realised now that the reason why his nose and chin were so close was because he didn't have any teeth in his head at all.

'My little brothers are always asking about you,' Julie put in. She was making it up, I think, to cover up her bad manners, but he actually smiled at her, as if to encourage her to carry on. ' "Where's Mr Punch?"

they keep saying.' She smiled back. '"We want Mr Punch!"'

He seemed to make his mind up about us then. He clapped his hands as a child might, delighted, and laughed his odd gurgling laugh. Then he jumped up and ran to the cupboard. He shook the door, and fumbled worriedly through his pockets.

'Do you want this, Mr Punch?' I asked, and handed him the key Matron had given me.

There must have been fifty shoe-boxes in that cupboard, all piled up one on top of the other, with sticky labels on. He ran his fingers down the labels and prised out one of the boxes. He carried it carefully over to the table, beaming at us. Surely he wasn't going to pay us for coming to see him? Kevin looked at me and mouthed 'sweets!'. Of course! His collection of Saturday treats! What a treasure store!

Mr Punch put the box on the table and beckoned to Julie to open the lid. We craned forward to watch. There was a rustle as Julie removed the layer of tissue paper. She gasped, and then started laughing. 'That's me!' Mr Punch laughed with her. 'That's me and our little ones!'

She lifted out of the box a little family group, all modelled in plasticine. The figures stood together on a grey slab, like paving-stone, and the tallest of them stood four inches high. It was easy to see it was Julie – long yellow hair in strands, blue jeans and a red sweater – even the white scarf and gloves her Barbie had knitted her last Christmas; their Robert, in his Everton track suit; and David and Matt in dungarees, and howling by the looks of them. They had little patches on their knees

and tiny blue shoes with their stripey socks bulging over them. He'd varnished and varnished the plasticine till it was quite hard. We couldn't get over the details.

'Look at our David's feet!' Julie giggled. 'He does, he stands just like that!'

'Look at your hair, though!' I marvelled. 'That little strawberry slide of yours, even. Look at the size of it!'

Mr Punch brought out another box. Eddy and Lesley, the snotty-nosed twins from down our street, scuffing each other and laughing their heads off, shoe-laces un-done and denim jackets spattered with badges. He opened more and more boxes for us, and we recognised all the children of the town as they came out of their hiding-places – babies crawling and little ones running and falling and pointing and hiding behind lamp-posts. Me and Julie sitting eating ice-cream sundaes, Kevin

67

with his paper-bag pushing his bike, Weird George with his spiky hair and big lobster red hands, and Marie and Andrew Wood, the very image of them, sharp little noses and kipper feet. The table, the bed, the chair and the floor were covered with tiny bright little figures and shoe boxes and tissue paper and Mr Punch had his strips of plasticine, showing us how he rolled them to shape them, when the matron walked in.

'What a mess, Mr Deacon!' she scolded. 'Your room's a tip. You must be the untidiest man I ever met.' But she winked at me, and Mr Punch took no notice of her at all.

'He's like a big kid!' she laughed. 'I think that's why he loves kids so much! He's still one himself. He can't have enough of their company. Loves kids!'

She looked fondly round at the mess in the room. 'Come on, Mr Deacon, get tidying!' she said. 'No tea for you till you've cleared up. That's the rule, as you very well know.'

'We'll help him,' Julie said. 'Shall we bring you the key back?'

The matron shook her head. 'No, he'll be all right now. I had to take it off him. He was in such a depression a few weeks ago, I caught him trying to smash them up. Imagine that! He won't do that again now, will you, Mr Deacon?'

Before we left we arranged to meet Mr Punch in the park the next Saturday. The matron shooed him off to the dining-room for his tea, and then took us into her office. 'You mustn't tell anyone about this model,' she said, taking a shoe-box out of her cupboard. 'As far as I know, it's the only adult he's ever done. It's my favour-ite.'

She lifted out a figure in a green overall, a duster in one hand and leaning on a vacuum cleaner. The face was bonier, much bonier, and the eyes much more protrud-ing, and the sarcastic twisted mouth much more cruelly curled than ever the real person's could have been, but we recognised her all right: Nicola Winkle's Auntie Rosemary.

'He kept this one in the top shoe-box,' the matron laughed. 'And her curiosity must have got the better of her one day, I suppose. She handed her notice in pretty quick!' She put Auntie Rosemary back into her box, put the box in the cupboard, closed the door, and locked it. 'No, don't let anyone tell you there's anything wrong with your Mr Punch,' she said, closing the lid down firmly. 'He's all there!'

4. Ganny Vitches

The woman who lived in the house next door to us was known as Ganny Vitches. I've no idea who first called her that. She wasn't really old enough to be a proper granny, and she had trouble with her w's, and she hated kids. She had always lived there. Her father died when I was about three, and she gave up her job as auxiliary night nurse at the Cottage Hospital to keep an eye on her mother, who must have been nearly seventy. Her mother obviously couldn't stand her, though, and after twelve months she ran off with the insurance man. Ganny was left behind complaining about all the sacrifices she'd made. I'm not sure what she meant by this – she hinted to my mum that she could have married a very handsome doctor, but I'm sure she was mistaken. She had back trouble, and walked so straight I thought she would break in half if she ever tried to sit down. Her hair was thin and straight and screwed up tight as a ping-pong ball on the top of her head, more like a big yellow boil than anything else. She said acid things about people in a very loud voice so they couldn't help hearing. My mum said she nearly died of shame if ever Ganny

Vitches trapped her into conversation on the street corner and any of her friends saw her. It was most unfortunate for us that she lived next door. If she heard my mum going into the yard to the bin or to put washing out she'd come out for conversation, and Mum would see the yellow boil coming along the top of the wall and duck down quick and crawl back on her hands and knees into the kitchen pretending that she'd dropped some pegs.

I used to spit on her door when I went past. All the kids did. We knew she hated us, anyway. You'd only to start skipping on the pavement or bounce a ball once and she'd be at her window, shouting at us: 'Go avay, vill you! Break some other body's vindow. Shoo off!' Then she'd prise open the top of her window and stick

her head through it sideways. 'I hate you silly kids!' she would hiss. 'Come closer and I'll vollop you!' If she was really mad she'd suddenly leap out of her front door and lunge out at you, and if you happened to be standing within reach you got your hair pulled. Kevin lived the other side of her and he was always losing balls over her back wall – he never got them back. She used to burn them, and you could hear her choking and coughing over the horrible fumes, but she'd rather do that than give them back.

One night I was singing my head off in the kitchen and she started banging on the fire-back – that's how we used to communicate in our street. She always does it when I'm singing, but I don't think it's my voice. I think she can't bear people to be happy – it gives her heartache. My granpa was like that when Nan died.

I sang a bit louder because I didn't feel like shutting up, and then I went into the pantry to get some potatoes for tea. That was when I found the mouse. He was sitting on the second potato that I picked out of the sack. I shouted to Mum to come and have a look.

'Mum! A mouse! Sitting on a potato!'

'Is it dead?' she asked, and instantly I dropped them both, mouse and potato, back into the sack.

'Oh, Mum!' I gasped. 'He is! I thought he was alive at first!'

'Poor little thing,' she said. 'He must have been squashed up in that sack for at least two weeks. We'd better get him out, though. Can't leave him to rot in there. D'you know, I can smell him! I thought there was a funny smell in this larder!'

72

I could smell him too, now she came to mention it. A real sharp smell that crept down your nose and stuck in the back of your throat.

Mum dragged the sack into the kitchen to get a better look. He was jammed in between two large potatoes, his head sticking up pertly. She picked one of the potatoes out and immediately more rolled down to protect the mouse. I did the same, and more potatoes rolled down. We jiggled the sack round, and still the mouse stayed upright.

'It's no good,' Mum said at last. 'I could pull him out by his tail, Bee, if he was the other way up. But I can't bring myself to pull him out by his head. Can you?'

I knew what she meant. I wouldn't have minded if he was alive, but I couldn't put my fingers round his dead little face and pull. Besides, he was stuck fast. His head might come off. Then what? Pull him out by his little hands? What if they came off too?

'Mum,' I said, closing the sack up suddenly. 'Shall I go and fetch Julie? She's bound to know how to do it.'

Julie's house was full of guinea-pigs, and they were always having babies. She must have had to get rid of dead ones. Their parish priest sat on one once, and squashed it. It wasn't his fault, you don't expect to sit on a baby guinea-pig when there's only one good arm-chair in the house. It must have given him an awful fright. But I'm sure Julie had had to get rid of that one – her dad had fainted, I know that. He's very squeamish. Anyway, Julie was having her tea when I went round, but she promised she'd come over as soon as she'd finished.

By this time we'd decided to have spaghetti with our sausages, and we'd just started to eat them when Julie came over with their Robert and a fishing-net. They soon got the mouse out, and we all held our noses and inspected him. He was a sweet little thing, but pretty mucky, dusted with dry earth, and he smelt stronger than a fish-cart.

'Take him out now,' Mum said. 'Bury him somewhere.'

But as soon as we got outside we knew what we wanted to do with him. Robert did it. He picked him up by his tail and whirled him round in the air. 'Harum scarum maggotty mouse. Put a spell on Ganny's house.' Mouse shot like a stream-lined sparrow over the wall and landed with a splat in Ganny Vitch's yard.

She was knocking on the fire-back when I went back into the kitchen.

'Bother her!' Mum said. 'Give her a song, Bee.'

I sang the National Anthem up the chimney, so she wouldn't feel so bad about having to stand up all the time, and that started her banging in real fury.

'She's applauding!' I said. 'Shall I give her an encore?'

Mum laughed. 'Perhaps you'd better pop round and see what she wants,' she said. 'She'll never shut up. She's not usually as persistent as this.'

Sometimes she would knock if she wanted to borrow something, or to ask me to run up to the shops for her. I knew what she wanted this time all right. She wanted to pull my hair because we'd sent the mouse over. She'd have heard us out in the yard. Pity it didn't hit her. I thought of twenty five different excuses and still Ganny

kept on knocking and in the end Mum pushed me out. I wish I had younger brothers and sisters. It's not fair. I always have to do everything. But I wasn't going in that house to have my hair pulled. I stood outside her door for a bit and then I shouted through the letter-box, 'My mum says will you stop banging, she's got a head-ache.'

I went back into our house and tried to sneak upstairs without Mum seeing me. 'What did she want, Bee?' she shouted.

'Her clock had stopped. She wanted to know what time it was.'

It wasn't long before the banging started again. Mum came up to my room.

'Are you sure you went round there?'

I confessed about the mouse. 'But it wasn't me who chucked it, Mum. It was Robert. So why should I have to go round and have my hair pulled?'

'Well, she's not going to shut up till you *do* go round, that's for sure, and I can't be doing with that racket much longer, it gives me the willies. Shall I come round with you? She can tell you off if she wants to, you little monkey. You should have more respect for a dead mouse. But if she tries pulling your hair I'll pull hers off, boil and all.'

Ganny Vitches didn't come to the door, but doors are always open in our street till dark comes. Mum pushed it open and marched in, ready for a fight. Ganny Vitches was bent in half over the empty fire, rapping on the side of the grate with a poker. She turned round when she heard us, kind of swivelled on her hips, and lifted her face up to us. She was white with pain.

'It's my back, Mrs Horton,' she gasped. 'It feels like it's snapped.'

'You've slipped your disc, love,' Mum said. Her voice was suddenly gentle with real sympathy. 'What a good job I heard you knocking.' We helped her slowly over to the table so she could lean on it, and Mum slipped a warm coat over her shoulders. Then I was packed off to fetch the doctor. I've never been so scared in my life.

Ganny Vitches was straightened out at the Cottage Hospital and then sent home to sleep on a board on the floor for a few weeks. A nurse came in twice a day to wash her, and we'd hear Ganny moaning away in that whiney voice of hers. If I pressed my ear to our wall I could hear every word they were saying, and I used to listen just to make sure she didn't tell about the spell we'd put on her.

But the nurse was only there half-an-hour. She needed more looking after than that. We sent Kevin with a message to her mother, who lived in the smart new estate over the railway lines, and she sent him back with a note that had roses on the front and smelt of peardrops. Mum read it out to her.

> 'Dear girl. I had nearly fifty years of your moaning. I've got a new life for myself now with a dear man and a lovely view of the allotments, and I'm not coming back. Sorry to hear you've been poorly though.
>
> Your loving mother.'

'Oh,' moaned Ganny Vitches from her sickbed on the floor. 'She is a vicked cat. After all my sacrifices. If my father vas alive she vould never dare say that. I am poor, sad, unhappy and deserted girl.'

She had no-one, and as we were the next-door neighbours who shared the same chimney because our fires backed on to one another's, ours was the responsibility for looking after her. But Mum was working at the laundry all day, and I was on half-term. It just wasn't fair.

'Just pop in once a day,' Mum said. 'Make sure the room's warm enough, do any shopping she wants, and make her a little bit of something for her lunch. It won't kill you, it'll do you good.'

I still don't see why my mum thought it was all so funny. I wasn't going to let Robert and Julie get away with it, though. I made them come in with me the first morning. She started shouting at us as soon as we opened the door. 'Close that door. That draught is like a knife in my bones. Vipe your dirty feet. Don't bang that door, it goes right through me! Oh you vicked children, how you stamp your feet. Valk gently before you break up my body vith your stamping.'

We stood in a silent ring round her, looking down at her ghastly white face and her thin hair that was all straggled out like pale spiders' legs on her sheet. We could spit on her from here, I thought, and that cheered me up. 'We've come to see if you'd like any shopping doing,' I said.

'Shopping? Can I trust you, that's the trouble. It's eggs I vant, but don't let him carry them, he'll drop the lot. And don't go to that supermarket, I don't vant their rubbish. And bring me a receipt so I know I get the right money back. And don't take all day neither.'

We backed away, ignoring the pound note she was holding up to us. 'I'm not going,' said Julie. 'My mum wouldn't talk to me like that, why should she?'

'Shall I put another spell on her?' said Robert. His eyes were shining with importance.

'You shut up about that spell or I'll tell Father McEvoy about you,' I snapped. I was worried though. I'd promised my mum we'd look after her, but at the same time I agreed with Julie. 'I'm going to talk to her,' I said. 'But you've got to stay with me. Right?'

We went back to the long figure stretched out on the floor. I felt quite powerful, standing over her like that. She looked quite frail, suddenly. 'The doctor says you'll always have back trouble now, on and off,' I said casually.

She sighed, prepared for a good moan. 'Oh, my Lord yes. It is my cross I have to bear. Sometimes pain, sometimes not pain. But never like this before. Never again, I hope.'

'Oh, I should think it will be,' I said. 'My mum says a bad back is like a broken tulip stem. It never mends, you know. Does it, Julie?'

Julie shook her head solemnly. 'It gets worse every time it goes. My dad's slipped his disc three times now. . . .'

'But you dad's lucky – he's got your mum to look after him. He couldn't manage without someone to look after him.' I looked down at Ganny. 'That's your problem.

Your mother won't come. My mother can't. And we're going out to play.'

'But my eggs!' she gasped. 'Vy won't you get my eggs?'

'Because we don't do favours for someone who pulls our hair and shouts at us. You're a nuisance. My mum nearly didn't bother to come round the other night because she's sick of you banging on the fire all the time. She only came because I was scared of you. You could have been dying, and she still mightn't have come. And I wouldn't have come on my own, if she'd been out, because I thought you were going to pull my hair.'

Julie was staring at me as if she'd never seen me in her life before, and Robert's eyes were wide with terror. I was dying to say something about his spell, but I kept it back. Things like that are better kept secret, especially from grown-ups. I glanced back at Ganny Vitches, but I couldn't bear the look on her face. Was it pain, or was her face crumpling up to cry? I didn't want to know. 'Come on Robert. Come on Julie,' I said. 'Let's get out before she tells us off again.' We turned quickly out of the room, and opened the door.

'Vait!' she shouted. We waited.

'Please!'

So we fetched her eggs for her, but when we got back we just stood round her holding the eggbox and the change and the receipt until she said 'Thank you,' and then we left the eggs where she could see them on the edge of the table until she said in a tiny voice, 'Vill von of you cook an egg for me? Please?' We quite enjoyed ourselves that day, and when she thanked us and asked us if we would be able to come again the next day we agreed quite happily. Before I left she asked me to check that her back gate was locked, and when I went out into her yard I suddenly remembered the mouse. It was still there, its bones sticking out now at odd angles, and its head loose. It was lying below the wall that divided her yard from Kevin's. I found a piece of loose slate and went to scoop it up, when Kevin opened his bedroom window and grinned down at me.

'You've found the mouse, then?' he asked.

'What d'you mean, found it?' I asked.

'Someone chucked it into our yard the other night,'

he said. 'My mum thought it was a bat, the way it came flying over. So I chucked it into Ganny Vitches' yard. Put a spell on her, I did.'

I was glad Robert wasn't there. I was quite sure second-hand spells didn't work. But I wasn't going to leave Kevin crowing, with Ganny Vitches stretched out on the floor and us three tired out with all the chores we'd been doing just to teach her to say please.

'Ganny Vitches could do with some coal fetching in, Kev,' I said. 'Will you come do it for her please? She'd be ever so grateful.'

'You're joking,' he laughed. 'She's never grateful for anything, that one.'

'I am not,' I said. 'Just you come and see for yourself, Kevin Proctor. It's magic, honest.'

And while I was waiting for him, I lifted the little mouse very gently, carried him carefully across the yard, and popped him in Ganny Vitches' bin.

5. A Slice for Peggotty

On good evenings we'd sit on our steps gossiping, doing the veg for tea, and our mums would stand leaning on the doorways with cups of tea in their hands, calling across to each other, and waiting for the bread cart to come round. It was driven by an elderly chap called Wallo, and pulled by Peggotty, his horse. Peggotty and my mum got on really well together – I don't know why, because she never liked animals in the house, never even let me have so much as a jarful of caterpillars. If there was any bread over from the day before Mum would put jam on it and save it for Peggotty, and the horse came to expect this little treat, and though she was pretty slow at getting about she would gallop past the last few houses on the street up to ours, and stamp on the step. If she didn't get what she wanted soon enough she'd come right in, or as far as the cart would let her, snorting and tossing her long head back till she got her slice. I didn't like to be the one who gave it to her, though – I didn't like to feel the flat slap of her wet mouth across my hand, or to hear the solid chomping of her enormous teeth.

Wallo would shout and bully her from outside, and

she'd back out noisily and plod on up the street. Sometimes she'd leave a payment for the bread and jam in a big steaming dollop on the pavement outside, and I'd have to shovel it into a bucket and put it into the back yard for Dad to take to his allotment. I didn't mind doing that.

But what we really liked to do was to sneak a ride on Peggotty's cart. She knew her round so well that she could have done it on her own, and as ours was nearly the last street to do Wallo often settled down for a snooze on his way back to the bakery, and left her to it. We used to sneak up behind them as they reached the end street and Wallo was too dopey to notice, and one by one we'd jump onto the cart. Sometimes there'd be as many as twelve of us, all jigging about and clinging on to each other as the cart swayed and lurched, while Wallo dozed with his chin on his chest and the reins slack in his hands. All of a sudden Peggotty would balk at having so much extra weight to pull, and she'd suddenly stop dead, no matter where she was. Wallo would topple sideways and wake up with a yell, but by the time he'd got his wits together we'd be off, tumbled or jumped or pushed or yanked, haring for home as if there was a prize for the winner, and Wallo would be shouting after us, 'You'll pay for this one day! You cheeky little monkeys!'

I was waiting out for Peggotty one afternoon when Kevin came round with a note-book and pencil and sat down on the step next to me.

'I'm doing the list for Saturday,' he said.

'What list?'

84

'For our market stall. I'm organising it.'

I nearly cracked out laughing, because really Kevin was the last person who should be asked to organise anything, on account of his forgetfulness. He once left a pound of pig's liver in the library, and it was there all weekend because he couldn't even remember where he'd been on his way back from the shops.

'I don't know why everyone thinks it's so funny,' he grumbled. 'Anyway – what's your family giving?'

One of our ways of raising money for the swimming pool fund was by having a stall in the market on Saturdays. Every street did it in turn. The fund was doing amazingly well, because my mum had been pestering all the shops for money, and they were competing with each other to see who could give the most. Her boss from the laundry had paid an enormous amount to have his *'West's Whites are Best Whites'* sign put up in the new changing rooms. 'Tell people it's for a good cause, and they don't want to know. Tell them it's cheap advertising, and they can't give you enough!' Mum grumbled, with every penny she took. We'd been swimming there nearly every day, but the money for the roof just wasn't coming in fast enough. Even Marie was losing heart.

'We've only got about a thousand to get now!' said Kevin cheerfully, as if this was nothing. 'As long as we do it by Christmas, we'll be all right. So what's your house putting on the market stall?'

'I'll get some flowers and veg off my dad's allotment,' I promised. it was the sound of Peggotty clopping up the street that reminded me. 'What's everyone else giving?'

Kevin glanced down his list. 'Bits and bobs. I've got some books and records off our Mike, and Julie's just had some baby guinea-pigs, so she said we could sell those – have you seen them? All squiggy and squashed – I wouldn't buy them, they're horrible. Mrs Marriot's promised to make us some toffee-apples and Mrs Wood's giving us some jewellery – you know those puky sparkly rings she has? Everyone's giving us something – except, of course – *her*!'

'Oh, *her*!' I said. 'What d'you expect?' Nobody would think of asking Ganny Vitches anyway – I know I wouldn't have dared.

That evening I went down the entry with my dad's wheelbarrow to help Kevin to collect stuff for the stall. Clocks, pyjama trousers, an accordion, two china ducks, a flowered chamber pot, shoes, shoes, and more shoes. It was amazing what people were piling on to it, and, as far as I could see, it was all junk. Nicola Winkle was watching me, sitting on the top of her back wall.

'Is *she* giving anything?' she asked.

'Don't know,' I shrugged. 'I'm not asking her, anyway. I'd get my hair pulled if I did.'

'She's got thousands you know,' Twinkle-Knickers said. 'Thousands. My Auntie Rosemary said she won the pools the other week.'

She does get me down, Nicola. Once when I went to tea there she wore a white ballet dress all the time, one of those sticky-out ones, even to play out in afterwards. She said she was practising for when she went away to ballet school, where she'd be expected to wear it all the time. Even though I knew her mum had bought it for her at a jumble sale, and that she didn't even have dancing lessons, she said that. She's always been like that – I don't think she knows what she's saying. Once when I was in their back W.C. when I was little she kept throwing shrimps over the door at me because I was scared of them. She said my eyes would fall out before I was twelve if I didn't learn to eat shrimps. I suppose she's all right, really. She's good at rounders.

'Have you got anything to donate, Nicola?' I asked.

'It's not our turn. We're next week,' she said 'It's not our turn. We're next week,' she said haughtily.

'Go on,' I pleaded. 'I'm not doing very well here. If you give me something for ours I'll let you have all our left-overs for yours. What about your white ballet dress? It can't still fit you.'

'As a matter of fact,' she said, sliding back off the wall into her own yard, 'I've donated that ballet dress to the Liverpool Museum. It was worn by a famous ballerina who danced so beautifully that admirers threw flowers on the stage, and she skidded on a rose petal and broke her leg. She never danced again.'

I left Nicola Winkle to talk to the pigeons. I was much too busy to be bothered with her.

Our stall wasn't much of a success though, when Saturday came. We only sold one of Julie's guinea-pigs, and actually that was to her big sister Barbie who'd found life very dull without them. Weird George bought a little red pull-along trolley that had belonged to Matthew, and spent the rest of the morning pulling his tortoise round in it. Mrs Marriot's toffee-apples went pretty quickly, but come to think of it, George bought most of them, too. A woman in a fur coat spent a lot of time looking at Mrs Wood's rings, and after she'd gone a young man came over and showed some interest in them. He had tattoos on his hands and looked pretty shifty, really. I kept my eye on him. There wasn't really much else to look at, because our stall hadn't created a lot of attention. Perhaps people were getting fed up with them. They all seemed to have the same things on them, week after week.

'I wish we'd got something special to offer,' I moaned. 'Perhaps we'd better send Julie a message to bring her tap shoes with her and do a dance on the table top when she does her shift this afternoon. It'd make people look, anyway.'

'Specially if she fell off,' agreed Kevin, yawning. 'I'm fed up, Bee. And I'm starving hungry, and I've forgotten my sandwiches. Have you got anything to eat?'

'Only bread and jam.'

'Great!' He grabbed one of Dad's big doorsteps, oozing with blackcurrant jam, and sank his teeth into it as if he hadn't eaten for at least six weeks. I took one as well, and prodded it to make it juicier, and sucked the sides of it where the jam was squeezing out.

Suddenly there was a commotion from across the market-place, a drag of wheels, and a husky shout, and I saw Peggotty, with Wallo's bakery van, swinging from her Saturday stand at the edge of the market, clopping and clomping round the other stalls towards our table. 'Stop that horse!' shouted Wallo, hobbling after her, but she lumbered on with the bread cart trundling behind her, knocking fruit stalls flying in her wake, and scattering the startled shoppers. Her huge mouth was twitching, wet with expectation, as she headed towards us.

'Kevin! Watch out! She's after our jam sandwiches!' I shouted.

'Well, she's not having mine!' he yelled, and grabbed the rest of the packet and ducked under the table with it. Peggotty came to a disgruntled halt, snorted angrily, smelt the jam, poked her head underneath the table, and sent the whole thing flying.

I've never seen anything like it. Kevin's records shot out of their sleeves and went skittering down the gutter. Julie's baby guinea-pigs squealed a chorus of terror and dodged away from every hand that reached out to save them. Peggotty reared up and brought her hooves down again on the table, smashing it in half, and books, jars of home-made jam and chutney, shoes, rings, the flowered chamber-pot and my dad's onions all tumbled to the ground and ran their various ways. Peggotty pranced round, tipping the fish-stall, and Fish-May slapped Wallo across the face with a fillet of plaice for not controlling his horse properly, and I don't blame her. George, shouting 'Help! Help!', crawled through legs after the whimpering guinea-pigs, trapped them at last in his big lobster hands, shoved them into his trolley next to his tortoise and trundled them back home to Julie's.

Arms reached out in all directions. I recognised the tattooed fingers again, picking and pulling and lifting and stacking with all the others, but had no time to think of anything much except poor old Peggotty, who was

not to be calmed down, not even with the remains of the jam sandwiches. 'She's hurt herself, that's why!' Wallo shouted at me. 'Hurt her leg on that darned table of yours – and if everyone would shut up, then so would she, but how can you expect her to calm down with all this racket in her ears?'

At last we understood what he was trying to say, and pushed the remains of the table to one side. We stood back quietly to give Peggotty's flailing legs some space to strike out at, and at last she stopped, and allowed Wallo to coax her away from the stalls to a part that was quiet. She was limping, we could see, and now that she was calmed the spirit seemed to drain away from her.

'Come on, old girl,' Wallo coaxed her. 'Come on, my lovely lady. Let's get you home and warm, eh?'

By this time Julie and Andrew had arrived to take over the stall from us. We sat on the floor round the wreckage and discarded everything that was broken into cartons. What we were left with wasn't worth buying. Nicola Winkle looked on, gloating. Marie Wood came down, almost speechless with rage at the way we'd let our street down. 'I might have known,' she kept saying. 'If I left Kevin to organise it, it would be a disaser. I knew it. We'll end up with no money for the campaign, and our street will be in disgrace. And it was all our idea in the first place!'

She walked round and round us, yapping on like a dog that's trapped its tail in a revolving door, making sure that everyone knew that it wasn't her fault.

'Shut up, Marie *Wood*!' shouted Kevin at last, boiling red behind his freckles. He flung down the carton he was holding, so all the contents spilled out again, and stamped off.

We stood round, pretending there was something to sell, but knowing in our heart of hearts that the best thing we could do was to pile all the junk on Wallo's abandoned bread-cart and go home.

Suddenly Kevin appeared again, with no breath left in him at all and his arms piled up with shoe-boxes.

'Get a couple of big cartons, quick,' he panted. 'And put them right here, upside down. Marie – get a chair from somewhere.'

She ran off without a word, and when we came back with the cartons Mr Punch was there, breathless too, and loaded up like Kevin with shoe-boxes. Very gently he took out, one by one, his little bright plasticine models, and placed them on the upturned cartons.

'But Mr Punch . . .' I began, and he waved me aside as if to say, 'It's all right. I can always make more.'

Marie hadn't seen the figures before. It's funny how your own face, like your own name, leaps out at you from all the rest. She picked herself out straight away, and blushed at the way it showed off her kipper feet, and then laughed, because it was certainly very nice about the way she smiled.

'It's no good,' she said at last. 'I'm just going to have to buy it. It's beautiful! Well, you know what I mean. It is, though.'

Kevin smirked.

Mr Punch's little figures were irresistible. Even the most hardened mums, who slapped their kids in public and never bought them ice-cream unless they were on holiday were seen to come and come again, pick up, put down, and at last, smiling fondly, buy.

Kevin did the selling and Mr Punch just sat back and beamed, and you could tell by the way he was watching all the children who came up to the stall that he was storing up details of puckered up faces and pleading

looks to put on his next batch of plasticine models when he got back to the nursing home.

By the end of the afternoon the shoe-boxes were empty, except for the one that was in front of Kevin, and that was piled high with money that people had paid for the little models. I looked smugly for Nicola Winkle, remembering what she'd said about Mr Punch's shoe-boxes being stuffed with money; but she'd gone home nursing the little model of herself that she'd bought, and mooning over it at every street corner.

'Come on, Mr Punch,' Kevin said, putting the lid carefully on the box. 'It's your tea-time, I think. I don't suppose there'd be any bread and jam to spare at your place, would there? I'm starving!'

We others trailed back to our street. Weird George came to meet us, still dragging his little red trolley behind him. Marie bent down to tickle his tortoise and then squeaked in horror.

'George! Just look what your tortoise is doing! It's sitting on my mum's jewels! It's eating one of the rings!' She scooped all the rings out lovingly, polishing the big bright stones on her cardigan. 'My mum's beautiful jewels! How did they get there, anyway?'

Andrew coughed. 'I put them in the sale, Marie. I didn't think she'd want them any more – I mean, they are a bit nasty, aren't they?'

Marie was scandalised. 'Mum's jewels! Oh Andrew. All her beautiful rings! She'll kill you.'

'Well, no-one tried to buy them, anyway,' Andrew muttered, though I could tell he was feeling a bit ashamed. 'That proves how nasty they are.'

'Ah, someone did,' George said. 'But he gave them back to me when I was taking the guinea-pigs home. He said he didn't think he'd bother because they didn't look real.'

Marie's eyes were round with horror. 'The cheeky devil! Not real? My dad buys her these, a new one every birthday.'

George shrugged. 'Well, he asked me what I thought, and I said I thought they were horrible, so he said we might as well have them back.'

'The cheek of it!' Marie gasped. 'You'd better not let my mum hear you say that, George Nightingale. How much did he pay for them, anyway?'

We didn't say anything, any of us. We all knew that none of us had sold any of the rings at all. Someone must have pinched them when they were chucking round on the floor and then decided that they weren't worth pinching after all. But we kept that secret to ourselves. Poor old Marie, I thought. What a disgrace.

I was just settling down to my tea that night when there was a banging on the door. It was Wallo, and he was on his own.

'Come on,' he shouted, 'You've a pair of arms, and a couple of strong legs, and that'll do! Out you come, young lady!'

I followed him out, mystified. 'What's up, Wallo?' I asked.

'Nothing's up except a lame horse and a load of bread that wants delivering. Get your friends, if you've got any, and be quick about it.'

I ran round for the others, and we ran after Wallo, who was stomping off down to the bakery in Back Street, waving his arms to hurry us on. His cart was waiting, heaped up with bread. He swung himself on to it, grunting. 'Righto!' he sang out. 'Pull!'

So that was how we spent the rest of that day. Pulling Wallo and his delivery of bread round all the houses, till the evening sun grew dim, and the black swifts screamed overhead.

6. The Hermit of the Sandhills

Not long after he got locked in the picture house poor old Robert was in trouble again. I don't know how they manage it, that family. No wonder Mrs Mills always looks as if she needs five weeks sleep. I'd come home from my paper round and found our house empty. I couldn't understand that. There's always someone at home, always, this time on a Friday. I banged on the window and shouted through the letter-box and stood there feeling abandoned, out in the cold and the wet, when suddenly I heard my mum's voice shouting to me from over the road. 'Over here, you daft dumpling. Can't you see for looking?'

And there she was, standing inside Julie's window on the ledge, shouting at me through the top. That bottom window of theirs has been stuck since Julie's mum painted the house six years ago.

It's always a bit of a mess in Julie's house. I climbed over the guinea-pigs and all the toys on the floor and Julie made me a cup of tea while my mum explained that she was looking after things because Robert had had to go to the Cottage Hospital to be stitched up. I smiled at Julie sympathetically. There was always someone from her family getting themselves stitched up at the Cottage, or having a plaster cast put on or taken off, and it was always Julie's mum who had to take them there because Mr Mills always fainted at the sight of blood. He couldn't help it. Mum said he was upstairs now, lying down.

Mum went over to our house to get tea ready while I helped Julie to get some chewing-gum out of little David's hair. We'd just got the two boys to bed and Mr Mills had staggered downstairs and out into the rain for some fresh air when Mrs Mills came home. She looked terrible. Her hair had come out of its bun and was plastered onto her cheeks and neck, and when she took her coat off I could see that her blouse was spattered with blood.

'Where's our Robert?' Julie shrieked.

Mrs Mills pushed a guinea-pig off the easy-chair and collapsed into it. Her head sank back and she closed her eyes as if she'd gone to sleep.

'Mum, where's our Robert?'

I could tell by Julie's voice that she was scared. I was scared too. I wanted to run off home. Mrs Mills opened her eyes wearily. 'Oh, he's all right, love,' she said. 'He lost a lot of blood so they're keeping him in tonight. We can probably fetch him home tomorrow.' She shuddered, and pulled her cardigan across to hide the bloodstains on her blouse. 'He cried ever such a lot.'

I thought she was going to cry then. I liked Mrs Mills. I thought she was one of the nicest mums in the street, next to my mum, but you had to catch her between nine o'clock and four o'clock to see her at her best. I decided to get off home before she did start crying, and Julie came to the door with me.

'Will you come to the sand-hills with me tomorrow, Bee?' she asked.

'The sand-hills? What d'you want to go there for?'

'That's where our Robert cut himself, Mum said. He's not supposed to go there even, but he wanted to go last night when I took him to church, and I wouldn't let him. But then he must have sneaked off there, the little monkey. Will you come, Bee, after your paper-round? My mum's that worried.' She looked round at her mum, slumped back in her chair, her eyes closed again. 'Will you?'

My Saturday morning paper-round took me up the main road past the Catholic church. I shared that one with Kevin; we always met up by the church afterwards and walked across the sand-hills down to the prom, so we could come back the long way. I liked the Saturday morning round.

'Will you – ' she said again. I could tell that it really mattered that I did. I shrugged.

'O.K.,' I said, though I couldn't really see how we could help Robert or Mrs Mills by going to the sand-hills. 'See you at half seven by the entry.'

We had to pass the Cottage Hospital on the way to the sand-hills, and Julie and I sneaked up the drive and scuttled round to the men's ward under cover of the hydrangea bushes to see if we could see little Robert. So many of Julie's family had been in the hospital for one thing or another that she knew the routine of the place as well as she knew her school time-table.

'They'll have had their early cup of tea and temperature, and a quick wash, and they'll be sitting up in bed waiting for their breakfast. I think it's sausages and tinned tomatoes on a Saturday.'

We peered through the window. There they all were, like a shelf-full of broken dolls, all splints and bandages and striped cotton pyjamas, staring in front of them as if they were waiting to be wound up.

'There's your Robert,' I said. 'Doesn't he look clean?'

He was propped up on a pile of pillows between two patients with broken legs. I think the whole ward must have seen us waving to him before he did; in fact several old men waved back to us, as if they always had friendly visitors peering in at that time in the morning.

When he saw us Robert slid out of bed and came trotting over to us. We both started giggling because his hospital pyjamas were much too long for him and he had to keep stopping to pull his trousers up. He eased the window up a crack, and I pushed a roll of polo mints through. They'd been in my coat pocket a week and the wrapping was still soggy from the soaking I'd had the day before.

'It's great in here,' he said. 'All the old men have been giving me their grapes because they can't eat the skins – and guess what we had for breakfast?'

'Sausage and tinned tomatoes!' we all chimed together.

'Robert Mills, will you get into your bed this minute before you catch your death of cold. . . .'

We ducked down quick as the ward sister bore down on him, and when we raised our heads over the sill we were just in time to see him heaving himself up onto the high bed, his pyjama trousers round his knees, and runaway polo mints rolling across the floor like hailstones skidding on ice.

The sand-hills were between the hospital and the church, and as we walked across them we could hear a service going on. There couldn't have been more than a handful of people who'd made it there on that miserable Saturday morning, but we could hear their voices making the responses, rising and falling like waves, and somehow they seemed to fit in with that morning; the slack rain still drifting down from the low sky, car tyres slushing on tarmac, seagulls screaming.

We used to call the sand-hills moon mountains. The sands were so soft and fine that they used to clog your feet when you tried to run across them, with solid clumps of marram grass like stout tufts of hair growing in them.

It was evil, that grass. It snapped at your knees as you walked through it, and left a wound as deep as a knife-cut on your fingers if you tried to pull it. But it was great for making owl noises with. Sometimes when the tide brought a wind with it the sand would fizz across your face, harsh as grit, but today the ground was sodden.

'What d'you think our Robert was doing down here on his own, Bee?' Julie said. 'That's what puzzles us. And what could he have cut himself on?'

'What about the shelters?' I said, suddenly. 'We always used to come down and play in them, didn't we?'

They were great, those shelters. Some people said they were air-raid shelters, left over from the war. We used to use them as dens, because some of them had ladders you could shin down. We used to spend hours there, even though they were damp and smelly and a bit scary, too. One of them caved in once, and all the sand from the dune over it tumbled in like water. There was a terrible panic that day because someone said Johnny Shepherd had been playing there when it happened. Men came down with spades and shovels, and women were on their knees, scooping out handfuls of sand, but the more they scooped it out, the more the soft sand from the sides trickled in. The men dug and dug without saying a word, and the women sobbed to themselves, and we were all huddled round, not daring to speak, thinking of that yellow weight all pressed down on Johnny Shepherd, when suddenly someone noticed that he was standing watching as well. He'd been to his grandma's and they'd both come down to watch what was going on. They boarded the shelters up after that, and I suppose we were all told to stop playing there. It didn't look much of a playground today, with the rain scything across it and those voices from the church wailing and drifting like graveless ghosts.

Julie had wandered off, and suddenly she called out from the top of one of the moon mountains that she'd found a shelter with its lid off. I ran up it to join her, and sure enough the metal lid at the top of the shelter was lying to one side, and blackness yawned below us.

'I bet he fell in there,' she said. 'I bet!'

'But how would he have got out, Julie? The top of

this ladder's missing.'

We were lying flat down on our bellies in the squashy sand, with our heads hanging into the round black mouth of the shelter, when suddenly from deep beneath us came a great shout, throaty and echoey and rumbling round and round. We both flung ourselves up, yelling, and loped across the clogging sand and the stinging grass till we were out of sight of the shelter and the church and off the dunes altogether by the slipway, where the brown sea flung itself at us as though it was trying to catch us in its arms.

And coming along the beach towards us was Weird George, guiding his bike along with one hand and dangling a wriggling fish from the other. 'Do you like my fish?' he shouted, though he was barely within earshot.

'Where d'you get it, George?' I shouted back.

'Caught it!' he yelled proudly. He brought his bike up against the slipway railings and held the fish up for our approval. 'I was watching Fish May up at the other end,' he said. 'Her Ted had just put a new catch of fish on her cart, and they were still alive. One of them jumped right off and I ran up and caught it! Then Ted said he'd never seen anyone catch a fish that way before and I could keep it.'

'Are you going to eat it, George?'

'Oh no. I like it.'

We knew very well that George had once eaten his pet goldfish because he didn't like it. We'd seen him do it. He held it up thoughtfully, watching it flap. 'I thought it might make a nice present,' he said.

George liked giving presents. He didn't really care

what he gave you, if he liked you.

'I hope you're not thinking of pushing that thing through *my* letter-box,' I said. I know it sounds ungrateful but you have to be firm with him.

He shrugged and shoved the fish into his back pocket. Its tail-fin waved forlornly. 'I *might* be able to sell it.' He jerked his head towards the sand-hills, and winked. 'But keep that to yourselves.' He looked round quickly to make quite sure no-one had overheard him, and clicking his knees back into their cycling position, wobbled off.

'Julie,' I said, gazing after the squishy marks George's tyres had made on the road. 'D'you dare come back to the sand-hills?'

'I dare if you dare, Bee,' she said. 'But only to make sure George doesn't fall down that shelter, too.'

By the time we got back to the sand-hills George was running back off them to where he'd left his bike propped. 'George!' I shouted. 'Where 'you going?'

He jumped on his bike without looking round. 'Back home quick!' came his voice. 'That's where.'

We pulled each other across and up the moon mountain where the shelter was. Then we stopped. There wasn't a sound now, except for the wailing gulls. We both dropped to our hands and knees and crawled forward, so that the marsh grass squeaked as we pressed it down. I could tell by the way Julie was running her tongue across her lips that her mouth was as dry as mine was, in spite of the rain soaking over us, in spite of it washing through our hair and our clothes as if it intended drowning us out there on those cold dunes. And I could tell by the way she held her head to listen that she could hear nothing except the powerful drumming of her own bloodbeat in her ears. Perhaps we wouldn't bother, we were both thinking. Perhaps we'd go and see Barbie instead. But you know how it is when you find a squashed hedgehog in the road, and you don't want to look at it because its insides are spread out and the bluebottles are humming on it, but at the same time you can't take your eyes off it? That's how we felt about that big black hole in the sand that had roared at us before.

And then I knew that I was braver than Julie because I stretched myself forward until I was flat on my belly

and heaved myself up that last slope till my head was next to the opening in the shelter. I could hear something all right, but it was the wind sort of chuntering to itself round the corners of the shelter, and the rain dribbling down into little pools. I pushed myself further down.

'Whoo!' I breathed experimentally. 'Whoo! Whoooo!'

'Bee, you'll fall in!' Julie said from outside. She clung onto my knees as I wriggled further down.

'Hoo-toodle-oo!' I called, louder this time, and feeling a lot better, and then the old air-raid shelter spoke to me again, and because I was more in than out, I heard what it had to say.

'I wish you kids'd stop staring in at me and making clever noises, and would fetch me a chip buttie instead.'

'Julie!' I gasped.

'What's he say? What's he say?' she shouted, leaning over me and nearly dropping me in.

'I said I'd be very grateful for something to eat, that's all. That's all I want.'

The voice grumbled round and round but it wasn't really a scary voice at all. It was a very cold and hungry voice, I thought.

'Someone just chucked a wet fish at me,' he went on. 'Well, it was very kind of him, I know, he's a good lad, but I'd rather have a bit of batter round it now, and a dredging of salt and vinegar.' He sounded so sorry for himself that I'd have given him my packet of polo mints, if I'd still got them.

'D'you always live down there?'

'I've only been here for a week, and it seems like a lifetime. And I'm not staying here much longer if it goes on like this, I can tell you.'

'Well,' Julie said. 'You ought to be ashamed of yourself, frightening people like that.'

'Crikey!' said the voice. 'It was you who frightened me. Can't see I'm doing any harm to anybody, stuck down here.'

'What are you doing, then?' I demanded. I felt quite brave now, being up top, and him being down there, and with him sounding so sorry for himself as well.

'If you must know,' he said forlornly, 'I'm hiding.'

Suddenly there was another noise, from behind us this time, and Julie jumped up and dragged me out of the hole feet first.

'And what's supposed to be going on here, I'd like to know. Sunday school outing?' Constable Harvey was clambering over the dunes towards us. Julie squinted nervously, and down below us the voice moaned.

'This place is swarming with kids today,' Constable Harvey went on. 'I just don't know what's up with kids these days. Isn't the telly good enough for you on a day like this?'

I don't know why, but I kept the voice to myself, and so did Julie. 'We're just looking for someone,' I managed to get out.

'Aye, well, I've just sent him packing, too. He said *he* was looking for his bike. Down an air-raid shelter, I ask you! I've just this minute told him to get back home quick, and that's where you're going too, this minute, before your dads send for the life-boat to rescue you from the weather. Come on now, scarper!' He shooed us off through the church-yard and up to the main road and I don't know why but we laughed like hens all the way home.

Robert was home when we got back, and rejoicing in

all the attention he was receiving. We couldn't wait to get him on his own. We made the excuse of taking him across the road to Mrs Marriot's front room shop to buy him something, and he skipped across with us, king of the day, holding up his sleeve so everyone would appreciate his bandaged arm. Bonfire toffee we were getting him, that jammed your teeth together and sent rich juices trickling down your chin, and made the sides of your face ache with sweetness. We let him hover over the tray, while Mr Marriot sat in the corner of the room poking the fire with his walking-stick and waving the smuts away from the trays of cakes and sweets that Mrs Marriot had made. Really, he was keeping an eye on us to make sure we didn't pinch any.

'Are you buying or smelling or what?' Mr Marriot said at last. Julie edged Robert away from the toffees.

'Where did you cut yourself, Rob?' she asked.

'On the sand-hills. I fell over.'

'I've never heard of anyone cutting themselves like that on the sand-hills. Tell me the truth, or you don't get any sweets.'

Robert sniffed. The tray of toffee sent warm sweet smells drifting up to us. The chunks were big, and sticky round the edges – you could tell because they had the impression of Mrs Marriot's fingers where she'd pressed down to cut them.

Julie turned away from the tray. 'I fell down a hole,' Robert blurted out desperately.

We watched Mrs Marriot prise up the toffee with a palette knife and slide it into a cone of paper. She popped a piece into her own wet mouth.

As we came out of the house shop Julie handed me a piece. It was so big that you had to curl your tongue up round the edges of it, and suck, or clam your cheek with it. Robert watched while Julie chose a piece for herself. 'How did you get out of the hole, Rob? And how did you get home?'

'I've got a sort of friend there,' he muttered.

That wasn't enough. 'Sort of?'

And that was how Robert, in exchange for the rest of the bag of toffee, told us the story of Fingers Finnigan, who had rescued him from the picture-house that Saturday, and how Robert had seen him the other day on the sand-hills, when he came home from his little school next to the Catholic church.

'But what's he doing there?'

'He lives there, of course.'

'Don't be daft. Who is he?'

'He's a secret.'

'*Robert*!' Julie's hand clenched over the bag of toffees.

'If you must know, he's some sort of angel. I knew you'd laugh. You always laugh at me. It's not fair. He looks after people, and now I'm looking after him. I promised. I promised. You've not to tell, Julie!'

But we did tell Kevin, because we'd spent all our money on Robert's toffee, and we had to borrow some money to buy his angel a bag of chips. Kevin solved the problem for us. 'Just supposing, for the sake of argument, that he *is* some sort of angel,' he mused. 'And he lives on his own, down by the church. I'd say that makes him a hermit!'

'Hermit? Do they have them these days?'

'I don't see why not. And he can't be a flying angel, not if he wants chips. ....'

I didn't believe in all this for one second, but I did want to make sure that that poor shivering person in the drippy shelter got some food inside him, and it didn't seem to me to matter how he got it. Kevin agreed to buy the chips provided he could come and meet him, so we queued up in the rain outside Maisie's chip shop, and Robert bore the steaming bag in triumph down to the sand-hills, with the three of us trailing him like body-guards. We had to hold on to his feet, though, while he passed the chips down to Finnigan, and I was surprised when I saw the face that appeared half-way up the ladder. He was younger than I expected, and very bony, and he had tattoos on his hands. He seemed to be wearing one of those black leather jackets with studs on, but I couldn't be sure in all that darkness. I just started to say: 'Hey, I remember you ...' when he grabbed the packet quickly and disappeared down the hole, and the steam disappeared after him, with its tantalising vin-egary smell. His voice came up to us, clotted with chips: 'Crikey! This is the best meal I've ever had!'

I knew what he meant. Chips, on a damp day, drown-ing in vinegar in a boat of salty newspaper – they were better than anything.

Unknown to us, Finnigan's mother was at that moment putting a last stroke of lipstick on in front of the police-station window. She patted her perm, smoothed down the fur of her coat, smiled at her teeth in the glass, and took a handkerchief from her handbag. Holding it delicately to her eye so as not to smudge her mascara, she flung open the door of the station and stumbled in.

'Help me!' she cried.

Constable Harvey and Sergeant Crisp both dropped their sandwiches at the same time and helped her to a seat. Sergeant Crisp, who couldn't bear the sight of a woman in tears, hurried into the back to put the kettle on, and Constable Harvey, who had a sneaking feeling that he'd seen her somewhere before, patted her hand consolingly.

'Is there anything we can do, love?'

'My son!' she gasped. 'He's run away from home! He's been missing for a week, Sergeant. He's gone, the dear boy's gone, and I've no-one now. No-one. The family business is wrecked, Sergeant. His father and his brothers are away, and they've left him in charge of it, and now there's no-one left to run the firm. *I* can't do it, Sergeant. Oh, but I want my boy back. You will help me find him, Sergeant, won't you?'

She peeped round at him. Constable Harvey was moved. He blew his nose and hunted for his note-book. 'Name?' he asked gruffly.

She smiled. 'Beatrice.'

'*His* name.'

'Fingers.' She put her handkerchief away, quite recovered, and brought out a photograph.

'That's him, Sergeant, the dear boy, at five years old. The image of his father. But with my smile, don't you think? My smile.'

'Does he have another name?'

'Finnean.'

'And another one, perhaps?'

She sighed, and dropped her voice to a whisper. 'Finnigan,' she breathed, with lowered eyes.

Constable Harvey underlined the name. He knew it from somewhere. Where had he come across it before? Where had he seen her before?

'Any idea why he left home, Mrs Finnigan?'

'We had a little tiff, Sergeant. You know what young men are. It all began some time ago after he'd been to one of the Saturday matinees. He told me . . . he told me . . .' Real tears welled up this time, at the memory of it. 'He told me that he didn't want anything to do with the family business after all, Sergeant, and that he'd rather starve! Think of it! And finally last week he walked out with only a pork pie and two sliced loaves, oh, and a box of cream cheese triangles, out into the rain. Never to be seen again.' She recovered again as Sergeant Crisp put a cup of coffee in front of her, and sipped at it delicately.

'Thank you, Constable. So you see, I must have him back. What his father will say when he finds out, I don't know. He trusted him to keep me in the manner to which I've been accustomed. To abandon the family firm when it was doing so well! He'll destroy him, if he ever finds him again. My poor, beautiful, Fingers Finnigan!'

When at last she'd been persuaded to go home and find a more recent photograph, Constable Harvey looked at Sergeant Crisp and said, 'Remind me, Sergeant. Where've I come across the name Finnigan before?'

'Moved in from Liverpool last year. Family of jailbirds. There's Tricky Finnigan, doing five years, and his two lads, Winks and Tiptoe, doing two years each. In and out of prison like frogs in a pond.'

'So what's this family business she's on about?'

'Burglary. Jewels and furs, mostly. Not very good at it, I might add, but they keep trying.'

'And this one, Fingers. Has he ever been in trouble?'

'Not yet, Harvey. Not *yet*.'

Constable Harvey, walking home from the station that evening, and going over the conversation with Mrs Finnigan in his head, puzzled over the fact that she'd said her son had been to the Saturday matinee. That was an odd thing for anyone over twelve to do, he thought. And that jerked him into thinking about something else – he'd heard that little Robert had been locked in the picture house, and it had puzzled him ever since that a little scrap of six could have managed to climb out of that high back window without hurting himself, and yet could have cut himself badly enough to need half a dozen stitches on the sand-hills, of all places. It didn't make sense. It didn't make sense, either, that half the kids in the place had suddenly decided that there was nowhere better to play these days than the sand-hills, and were to be seen traipsing backwards and forwards at all hours, often smelling strongly of chips. As it was a wet night, and he could be sure of a cup of tea at Mrs Mills' house, he decided to start there.

I'd been there all evening. It was like a big party, with Kevin there too, and Julie's big sister Barbie and Kevin's big brother Mike. They had got married at the beginning of the summer and now they had come home to tell their mums and dads that Barbie was going to have a baby. I couldn't take my eyes off her. I wondered if it hurt, and I saw there was a plumpness and a brightness about her that I hadn't noticed before. I didn't want to go home. I never did when I was at Julie's house. Kevin and I set off together, but when we saw Constable Harvey coming down the entry we dashed back in quick, pretending it was raining too heavily, because neither of us wanted to miss anything.

Constable Harvey was delighted to see us all there together. 'I've come to have a word with your little scamp Robert,' he said. 'But I'll have a go at these three too, while I'm here.'

And that was when the memory of the boy in the shelter took hold of me again, like an icy draught creeping down my spine. I hadn't thought of him all evening. Angel, I thought dismally. Hermit! What idiots we were. There was only one reason why people hid in holes, and that was because they were wanted by the police. I didn't dare look at any of the others, and they didn't look at me.

Mrs Mills called Robert into the kitchen, and clanked anxiously with the kettle and the cups while Constable Harvey fumbled in his pockets. He suddenly found what he was looking for, dropped on his haunches and thrust a photograph in front of Robert's face.

'Who's this?' he asked. Robert burst into tears.

He couldn't get any more out of our Robert though, and I must say I felt proud of him, standing with his face clenched up in the middle of the kitchen, with wet nappies dripping on him from the rack, and his mum and dad and Constable Harvey and Barbie and Mike all standing round him, coaxing and threatening and questioning and shouting. Kevin and Julie and I stood behind them, not daring to move in case Constable Harvey picked on us, and when Robert looked between the grown-ups we promised him with our eyes that we wouldn't say anything unless he did. Finnigan was still Robert's friend, whoever he was.

It was a battle of nerves, but Robert won in the end, and Constable Harvey went off home without his cup of tea, and Kevin and I went back to our houses in silence, knowing we'd done a terrible thing in keeping information from the police, and not really understanding why we'd done it, either.

Fingers was in a bit of a state when we passed his breakfast of jam sandwiches down to him the next morning. He coughed and wheezed and spluttered and eventually let us understand that he'd lost his voice and he'd be very grateful for a bottle of cough medicine.

I was very worried about him. 'I wish you'd go back home to your mum,' I urged him.

'You should give yourself up to the police!' Julie insisted. 'Whatever you've done, you'd be better off in a prison cell, warm and dry, than down here.'

But his coughing drowned out his reply. I threw my gloves down to him, that I'd knitted myself, and Kevin dangled down his football scarf, but Julie said that he didn't deserve any more help from us, letting on that he was an angel when he was more likely to be an escaped prisoner. Robert hadn't anything that would fit him anyway, but he did chuck down a grubby handkerchief.

We trailed back home across the damp sand, not sure what to do.

'I think we should give him up,' Kevin said at last.

'I *know* we should,' insisted Julie. 'We're aiding and abetting a criminal, and that's against the law. We might all end up in prison.'

'But he's Robert's friend, and it's up to Robert to hand him over,' I pointed out.

'Robert's too young to decide,' Julie snapped. I could tell her conscience was bothering her. She doesn't usually lose her temper, and she was usually very fair.

'Robert,' I said. 'I'm a bit worried about your friend. He's not very well, is he? I think he'll get a lot worse if he stays down there much longer in this weather.'

Robert nodded. He looked really anxious, like a little old man with a lot of worries on his shoulders.

'In fact,' I went on carefully, 'If he doesn't come out soon, we're going to have to get a doctor to him.'

'He might have to go into hospital,' added Kevin.

'He might even die!' Julie hissed. 'And it'd be your fault. Is that what you want?'

Robert shook his head.

'But don't worry. We won't tell anyone, will we, Kev?'

'Course we won't. Not unless Robert wants us to. We promised.'

We waited outside the police-station while Robert marched in. I don't know if I could have done it, even now.

Robert looked all the way up to Constable Harvey's kind face and muttered: 'You know that boy you're after? He's down a shelter in the sand-hills.'

Constable Harvey paled slightly. Why hadn't he thought of that himself? 'Thanks, kiddo,' he said. 'I know a lady who'll be very pleased to hear that news.'

Tears blurted into Robert's eyes. 'I only told you because I want him to get better. Will you tell him?' He ran out and all the way home without saying a word to any of us.

We kept an eye on the sand-hills after that, and soon afterwards we saw Constable Harvey and a splendid lady with orange curly hair and a big fur coat heading that way.

'Who's she?' asked Julie.

'That'll be the one who reported him in the first place,' Kevin whispered. 'I bet he did a robbery in her house. Doesn't she look posh?'

'She's ever so upset,' I said, watching her stroking her cheeks with her handkerchief. 'It must be terrible to be burgled.'

We followed them down to the dunes in the wake of the curly woman's sharp perfume. Progress was slow because her stiletto heels kept digging into the soggy sand, and the wind seemed to have robbed her entirely of breath. She also had trouble keeping her perm in place. We flattened ourselves against the moon mountain as Constable Harvey made his way up to it, with the curly woman gasping behind him, and then we scrambled up it, dragging ourselves hand over hand by the marsh grass. Both my hands bled where the grass had cut into them, and my face stung where the sand whipped against it.

'Fingers Finnigan, I know you're down there. Will

you come on out now please?' ordered Constable Harvey, and it wasn't long before Finnigan, coughing, made his way up the ladder and was helped over the last part of it by Constable Harvey. It seemed to me that he was glad to be out of that dark hole at last, and out into air that was fresh.

But: 'Fingers! My beautiful boy! Come to your mother!' the curly woman shrieked, and Fingers looked round in horror and jumped right back into the hole again. We heard a bony crunch, a husky yelp, and then silence.

Constable Harvey understood everything, and so did we. 'Perhaps you'd better go back home, Mrs Finnigan?' he sighed. 'I'll have a talk with your son, and I'll be in touch with you later. . . .' Mrs Finnigan looked at him helplessly, angrily, then with a last troubled look down the hole that gaped like a grave between her and her son, she took off her stiletto shoes, rammed them into her pockets, and marched off home.

'It's all right, lad. You can come out now,' Constable Harvey called down. 'It's quite safe.'

But it was soon clear to us that there was nowhere else for Fingers to go when he did come out of the shelter. 'I'm not going back home,' he croaked, shivering, as he was being hauled up onto the sand again. 'I've done with her, and I've done with *them*, and I've done with the family business. Oh, I've had enough of my mother, and I don't care who knows it.'

I didn't blame him. She reminded me of melted ice-cream, that's all frothy and sweet and oozing out of its wrapper. 'Me dad says I'm a failure, and he's right.' He

sneezed. 'I might as well admit it.'

'But where can you go, son? You can't stay here....'
Constable Harvey said.

Fingers shook his head, and blew his nose on Robert's
grubby little handkerchief. His teeth jittered in his jaws,
and his eyes were streaming. Constable Harvey cast his
eyes round him as if he expected to find the answer to it
all written down on the sand somewhere, or scrawled in
the sky, and then he looked at me and remembered the
best person he knew of for sorting out other people's
problems. 'Is your mum at home today, Bee?' he asked.

Funny, but I had her in mind as well.

Mum put Fingers to bed in the spare room, and cooked
him a hot broth. She watched him as he dipped into it,
and when he'd wiped the last of the juices of the bowl
out with a thick elbow of bread, and was drifting back
into the blessing of clean sheets and soft pillows she said,
'What do you want to do most in the world, Fingers?'

He sighed with the luxury of the question. 'All I ever
wanted to do was to cook, Missus. Food, that's what I
like best.'

He spent the next day, still in bed, reading recipe
books, and plotting the week's meals. The day after that
he was in the kitchen, cooking things we'd never heard
of, and the house was warm with the smell of baking,
and pungent with spices. I hung round him, watching
the rapid movement of his fingers as he chopped and
sprinkled and pinched.

'Is that why they call you Fingers?' I asked.

He scratched his nose. 'Crikey, that's a laugh. My dad

thought it would encourage me to creep into people's pockets and be clever at fiddling with locks, if he called me Fingers. But they just froze when I tried – stuck out like great poky sticks for everyone to notice!'

By the end of the month Mum had brought in application forms for a catering course at the Birkenhead Tech. I had to help him to fill them in. The day he posted them, she told him to prepare a very special meal for Sunday, because she was inviting a very special guest.

We never have people to tea, except my grandad. What was the point, when all Mum's friends lived in the street anyway, and had their own families' teas to get ready?

'Who is it, Mum? Who is it?' I kept asking.

'You'll see,' was all she'd say.

'I hope it's not my mother,' Fingers kept groaning. 'She won't eat onions, or eggs, or anything fattening, or runny, or wobbly. . . .'

But it wasn't his mother. I couldn't believe my eyes when I saw who it was. Ganny Vitches, of all people, with a smile as sour as half a lemon and all her attention on her aching back. She followed my mother slowly into the kitchen and sniffed at the sight of Fingers fiddling round with the last flurried touches.

'Vat is the world coming to, I ask myself,' she asked us, 'Ven ve let hoodlums into our homes to do our cooking for us?'

Fingers only winked at her. He was used to that sort of talk, on account of his jacket and all those tattoos on his fingers. I must say it put me off my food at first, seeing those blue and red and green painted hands of his dipping in and out of the flours and fats he was mixing. 'Just you perch on that chair, Missus,' he said, 'and give that poor old back of yours a rest. It must be killing you.'

'Mum, what did you ask her here for?' I mouthed at Mum from the larder. 'She'll give us all indigestion.'

'No, she won't, Bee,' Mum said firmly. 'She's eaten up with loneliness, that's all that's up with her. She needs someone to take an interest in, and *he* needs someone to take an interest in him. They'll get on like a house on fire, you'll see.'

She was right. She's a witch, my mum. My dad's always telling her that. Everything happened so quickly and I was so busy carting plates round and being nice to people that I could hardly keep up with it, but what transpired was that Ganny Vitches was seen to go wet round the eyes at the taste of Finger's pastry, and to say that she had never tasted anything like it since her father died. Then Mum let out a series of things like wouldn't Ganny be better off with a bit of company in her house, and then that she missed cooking, she really did, she hadn't been able to get near the cooker since Fingers arrived, and last of all, with a deep sigh, that Christmas wouldn't be the same without grandad, but that we hadn't got a spare room to put him in any more. But she threw all this in very casually, in between plenty of cups of tea and slices of cake. Ganny Vitches kept sighing, so the crumbs of her plate rose and scattered, and then Fingers started on the story of his life, and how he couldn't stand women who fussed him like his mother did, and how he didn't think he'd be able to keep out of trouble unless he had someone keeping a stern eye on him.

'Vell,' said Ganny at last. 'If you vill cook for me like this, and don't pinch nothing, and don't vear those hoodlum things neither, you can have my spare room.' She closed her eyes. 'No-body else vill, for goodness sake. No-body else vill vant to come and see me.'

So Fingers moved next door, and we put all our junk in the spare room again. It was nice to hear Fingers whistling away in the kitchen next door when he came back from college at night, and Ganny, prattling away to him. They invited her mother up to tea sometimes, and Fingers' mother too, though Ganny thought she was an evil woman. But their favourite guest was little Robert. He was always there, and he usually managed to scrounge an invitation to stay to tea. Fingers' cooking was wasted on him though. Sausage and tinned tomato, that was all Robert ever asked for.

7. Presents

Christmas Eve, and lights in all the windows. Frost on the road, and the air piping cold, and the sky as bright as satin.

My dad bought a tree in Liverpool market at the last minute, and struggled home with it on the rush-hour train. They had to stand all the way, him and the tree. When I went down to the station to meet him off the train I stood on the bridge and saw Dad's bald head coming up the steps, and the tree with his trilby hat on. I knew then that he'd been to a works' party, and that he'd be in a teasing mood all night while Mum and I were doing the mince pies, and that he'd suddenly go off into a deep snoring sleep. Everyone was in a good mood as they walked up the road from the train – Mrs Wood walked up with us, loaded up with last-minute shopping.

'They say that woman next door to you is having a do tomorrow afternoon,' she sniffed. 'I don't know what the street's coming to, with women like her having do's.'

'First I've heard of it,' said Dad. 'And I'm sure you'd have been invited, Mrs Wood, if she was having one.'

Mrs Marriot opened her door so all the sweet, warm, wonderful smells of her kitchen snapped at us as we came up. For once she hadn't been boiling fish for her cats, so there was nothing between us and the hot breads.

'It's all half-price today!' she sang out, so we heaped our arms with warm loaves and nibbled the crusty corners of them, all three of us, on our way home.

Fingers came running down the street behind us. He bit the end off Mrs. Wood's french loaf, and planted a crumby kiss on her cheek. 'My, we are full of the Christmas spirit!' she perked coyly.

'It's a glass of wine and a piece of cake for you tomorrow,' he said, 'if you'd like to pop in for five minutes.'

'Well, thank you very much! What a surprise!'

'Ah well, I want to give Ganny a treat. I want her to have a real good time of it. I've got me mum coming to dinner – I think I can even put up with her on Christmas day. And all you kids have got to pop in too. Ganny's got something for you, so she'll want to see you. And I've got a special friend of yours coming to dinner as well, Bee.'

'Not Father Christmas!' I said sarcastically. I was still getting over the shock of hearing that Ganny Vitches was going to give us something for Christmas.

'Someone better than that – Mr Punch!'

I could have hugged Fingers then, if he hadn't been so tall, and I hadn't been loaded up with bread.

'It was Kevin's idea,' he said. 'I told him I wanted to give you all a present, but I haven't got any money, not a bean, and he said you'd all like to see Mr Punch tucking in to my cooking on Christmas Day.'

'He won't eat much, anyway,' said Mrs Wood. 'He hasn't got a tooth in his head.' I don't think she meant to be unkind, though. She just loses control of her manners, my mum says.

'Can we fetch him for you?' I asked quickly, to drown her out.

'You do, Bee, and after he's had his dinner, you pop in and have some ginger beer, eh? It's going to be like a great big party at Ganny Vitches' house. Think of that!'

We all did think of that, and laughed. 'We'll all take our shoes off before we go in,' I promised, 'so she won't forget herself and shout at us for messing up her kitchen floor.' I still didn't quite trust Ganny.

'It'll be the best Christmas I've ever had!' said Fingers, when we reached his door. 'And look! It's snowing!'

When I told Kevin about Ganny's present he was quite sure I'd been mistaken. 'Nobody changes that much,' he said.

But Julie thought we ought to buy a present for Ganny, just in case it was true. 'She's been the making of Fingers Finnigan, everyone says that.' Certainly it seemed as if he'd been living in that little front bedroom in Ganny's house all his life; and telling my mum awful jokes over the back wall while he hung Ganny's washing out, and tap-dancing in Ganny's kitchen while he was waiting for eggs to boil, because three and a half minutes exercise a day was all he had time for; and sending the most exciting smells through the window when he was trying out new recipes. It was quite true; she'd been the making of Fingers. And he'd been the making of her.

In the end we decided to buy her a little box of chocolates between us, but none of us dared to give them to her. The only person we knew of who'd never been in any sort of trouble with her was George, because he'd always had the sense to keep away. I wrapped the chocolates up and wrote 'From the S.P.C. gang – we're sorry we made fun of you'; then crossed the last bit out and took it over to George. He was standing in his entry singing carols, hopelessly out of tune and at the top of his voice, holding his face up so the snowflakes drifted into his open mouth.

'Look after this till tomorrow, will you, George?' I asked.

He tucked the parcel up his jumper and carried on singing.

I went to bed early that night, but I couldn't sleep. I never can on Christmas Eve. I was awake long after Mum and Dad had gone to bed. The silence was peculiar, hushed and dead; I could tell that the snow was heavy now. I looked out of the window. Everything was blanked out. The street was like a white field. Then I saw some people coming down from the top, trudging slowly, and talking quietly to each other. It was Julie's family, coming home from Midnight Mass. I opened the window.

'Hi, Julie?' I called. 'Is it good out there?'

'It's great! It's fantastic!'

'*Ssssh!*' said her mum and dad.

'Happy Christmas!' Julie shouted. 'Happy Christmas, everybody!'

I left the curtains open and crept back into my lovely warm bed. I lay watching the snow drifting down like stars loosened from the sky, buffing and kissing the window-pane, till my eyes were too tired to watch it any more, and without knowing it, I slept.

When we did a count-down at the end of Christmas Day, we found that Weird George had been the first person in the street to get up. He'd felt his stocking at about four o'clock, and eaten the top tangerine and blown some bubbles, and then at five o'clock he actually got up. The first thing he did was to take out the little parcel that I'd asked him to mind yesterday. It was still wrapped up in his jumper. He read the label. 'From the S.P.C. gang'.

'All my friends!' he thought proudly. 'A lovely Christmas present from all my friends!' He read the bit I'd crossed out. 'We're sorry we made fun of you.' And he nodded sadly. But it didn't matter now.

He opened up the chocolates, and ate them.

It was still snowing in the middle of the morning when I called for Kevin. We slithered and scrunched our way down to the nursing home on the prom to collect Mr Punch. The whole world was completely silent except for our voices and the suck and crunch of our Wellies. There was no traffic on the roads at all – no roads in fact. When we reached the prom the tide was coming in. The water was black against such whiteness, and seemed to stretch from here to the Arctic. The lights of the nursing home glowed warmly; the snow piled on the rail of the balcony made it look like a long white scarf wrapping the house up against the cold.

'We've come for Mr Punch!' shouted Kevin, almost before Matron had opened the door.

But she shook her head sadly. 'I'm sorry, love,' she said, 'but the snow's put a stop to that. It was a lovely idea, but that's that, I'm afraid. He'd never be able to walk that far in this weather. It's much too dangerous. There, I'm sorry, Kevin love. He'll be all right with us.'

We thought of Fingers' beautiful fat turkey sizzling away in the oven, and Ganny's kitchen bright with decorations. Mr Punch came down the corridor to us with his hat and scarf on, and Matron went up to him and very firmly led him back to his room.

'I'm sorry, Mr Deacon. There, there. You'll have to have an extra helping of Christmas pud. There's plenty of good grub here, you know.'

We stood helplessly in the empty hall, hating the snow, hating Christmas, and hating old age that snatched like a thief at special things.

'Don't worry, Mr Punch – you'll have your Christmas dinner with us, even if we all have to come here!' Kevin shouted.

Mr Punch didn't even turn round, just lifted his hand as if to say 'Don't you worry about me.' But we could tell by the droop of his head and by the sag of his shoulders how unhappy he was feeling. It would have been better if Fingers had never invited him in the first place. We trudged back home and into our street, that smelt wonderfully at every kitchen window of roast

128

turkey just browning on the outside, and herb stuffing swelling with hot juices.

'I couldn't eat a crumb,' said Kevin miserably.

Meanwhile Fingers had slipped out before doing the vegetables and the sauces to fetch his mother. It was the first time he'd been back home since coming to live at Ganny's, and as he turned up into the little street of white houses where his mother lived he felt again the old dread of being peeped at behind curtains and of neighbours shaking their heads and saying 'He's a bad lot, that lad. Like all the Finnigans.' And as he pushed open the little gate to his own front yard he felt a twinge of the old shame because he didn't have his pockets bulging with things that he'd nicked, as his dad and his brothers would have done. He heard Ganny's voice in his head, saying to him, 'If I think for von minute that you vant to act like a hoodlum, I push you out in the cold street for ever.'

He grinned to himself. Good old Ganny, he thought. She's like a bag of brazil nuts, all rattle and hard shell, and keeping all her niceness out of sight.

The door opened. 'Fingers! My beautiful boy!'

He groaned. 'Come on, mother. Let's get it over with. And put your Wellies on – it's wet out here.'

She peered out at the snow. 'Wellies! I'm not a Wellies woman, Fingers, as you very well know. I wouldn't be seen dead in Wellies.' She wore her fur coat over a silk dress, her hair was newly permed, and she stood in red stilettoes. 'Besides ... these are my only decent shoes now, Fingers. Nobody brings me pretty shoes now, what with the family firm closing down.'

'You'll have to come like that then, I suppose,' he muttered. 'Honestly, mother, you don't half show me up.'

He pulled her through snow that was almost up to her knees, and with every step she took one of her shoes came off, and she had to cling on to him while she rooted round for it and wobbled to put it back on. Trickles of black mascara oozed down her cheeks. Her perm flopped. Her fur coat stuck out in wet spikes, and beneath it the hem of her dress flapped damply. She sat down at last on a big clump of snow that could have been a gate-post or a motor-bike or a dog or anything, really, and sobbed. 'You go on without me, dear boy. I didn't mean to show you up. I wanted to look smart for you, Fingers, and all your new friends. I can't go anywhere looking like this.'

Her voice rose to a howl and bright beads of tears rushed to a bulbous blob on the end of her nose.

'I want you to come, Mother,' Fingers said, and surprised himself with his sincerity. He did. He wanted her to come. He thought of his vegetables, lined up in pans waiting to go on the stove. He thought of Ganny, grumbling because she'd known she'd have to see to it all herself, in the end. He crouched down. 'Hop on, Mother,' he said.

Mrs Finnigan blew the blob of tears off the end of her nose, hoisted her skirt above her knees, and climbed on his back. She clung grimly onto his hair, with her hefty handbag clonking across his face, and he bit back the tears of pain and slushed through the snow towards Ganny Vitches' kitchen.

'I'm proud of you, Fingers,' he kept muttering to himself. 'At long last, you've done something to be proud of.'

In her kitchen, listening to the turkey popping behind the oven door, Ganny was growing fidgety. Fingers had forbidden her to touch anything, but she knew very well that the potatoes should be in by now. She kept looking at them, all peeled and ready in the pan, and she kept peering out of the window to see how much the depth of snow had risen on the sill. It was swirling down fast now, and thick, and it was as if it was closing her off from the rest of the world.

'The silly hoodlum is stuck in a drift, I know it,' she muttered. 'And we'll all be choking on hard potatoes at dinner. Never in my life have I had hard spuds on Christmas Day.'

Suddenly she tipped the water from the potato pan into the sink, and carried them over to the cooker. She couldn't bend low enough to open the cooker door, so she had to do it with her slippered foot, curling the toe end round the knob, and pressing down. At last the door opened; hot turkeyed steam rushed into the kitchen. Ganny jumped back, sniffing deeply. 'Vonderful!' she sighed.

She wanted to put the potatoes round the bird, but again the shelf was too low down for her to reach properly. She bent down as low as she dared, and eased the shelf out with the tips of her fingers. 'Oh!' she groaned. 'Ooh! Aaah! Come out, you vicked shelf! Come *OUT!*' One last tug and the whole shelf shot forward, tipped down, and the roasting tin crashed to the floor. The turkey slithered off it and slumped, sizzling, on the lino, and all its precious juices trickled like reaching fingers under the cooker, round the legs of the table, and soaked into the mat in front of the hearth.

Ganny gaped at it. 'You interfering old baggage!' she whispered. 'Vy don't you leave things alone?'

She crept away from the steaming pile, backed onto the damp hearth-rug, and, still gazing at the turkey on the floor, reached out her hand for the poker. For the first time for weeks and weeks, she banged on the fire-back.

I was helping Dad with the sprouts at the time.

'Quick!' I shouted. 'Something's happened to Ganny Vitches!' I shoved my Wellies on the wrong feet and ran round, and George, who'd been hanging round in the fresh air because he felt a bit sick, ran in after me. He went skidding on the rapidly cooling grease on the lino, and nearly kicked the turkey into the fire.

'You shouldn't leave things like that lying around,' he scolded her, in a state of shock. 'It's dangerous.'

Ganny lifted her hands helplessly. 'Vat can I do? I can't lift him! The thing is too low down for me! Soon Fingers vill be home, and ve'll have hard spuds – hard spuds, mind, and no turkey at all! Beans on toast it vill be, beans on toast on Christmas Day, and he vanted it all so special.'

I couldn't help grinning, though I wouldn't have let Ganny see it for worlds. I turned over the roasting tin and, using a plate and a slice, scooped the turkey back into it. I shoved the stuffing back in, where it was beginning to ooze out.

132

'What if there's hairs on the floor?' George whispered. 'Yuk! Hairy turkey!'

'There's no hairs!' I snapped, feeling sick at the thought of it. 'Anyway, I'll wipe him over with a tea-towel now, to make sure. Just you wash this floor and shut up!'

I wiped the turkey all over, then I snuggled the potatoes round it, and shoved it back in the oven.

'There!' I said to Ganny. 'He's as good as new!'

She was perched, pale and stiff, on the edge of her high chair. 'I didn't see that,' she said weakly.

'Neither did we,' I grinned. 'We didn't see a turkey on the floor did we, George?'

'What?' he asked amazed. 'Didn't you see it, Bee? I did. I nearly fell over it. I still don't know what it was doing there.'

I nipped round to my house to get some hot fat from our oven to get Ganny's turkey sizzling again. My dad carried it round for me, and drained it across the turkey and the potatoes. I sprinkled some fresh seasoning on, and turned the oven up. Then Dad poured Ganny a glass of sherry, and within minutes her yellow face was pinking up, and she was tittering at the thought of it all.

'Imagine if Fingers had been spying through the vindow at us!' she giggled, glancing round to make sure he wasn't. 'And that horrible mother of his! She vould be scandalised.'

'Ah well, we've all got to eat a ton of dirt before we go, as they say,' Dad said, stretching his legs out comfortably.

'Dirt,' repeated Ganny, her giggles spiking suddenly.

'There is no dirt on my floor, Mr Horton. Fingers vashes it vith his own hands every day. I keep my eye on that young hoodlum. Crikey, I do!'

George handed Ganny the soggy floor-cloth and backed towards the door, not intending to be involved in any argument. He hated to hear people raising their voices, because he was never quite sure whether they were shouting at him or not. 'I'd better be off now,' he said.

'Ah, just von moment. I've got a present for you children,' Ganny said.

Dad choked on his sherry, but she ignored his terrible manners. 'You might as vell take it now and be done vith it. Vell, vot you vaiting for? It's in the larder. Take it out and play vith it, and be out my vay.'

George brought it out. It was a sledge, pretty old, but beautifully made.

'My father made it me ven I vas little girl,' Ganny said softly. 'And I kept it all these years. Vy? I don't know. I'll never sit on it now, for goodness' sake!'

George sat down on it, quite overcome.

'George,' I whispered to him. 'Go and fetch Ganny's present.'

'What present?' he whispered back.

'You know. The one I asked you to look after last night.'

He look puzzled. 'That parcel?'

'Yes,' I said impatiently. 'Ganny's Christmas present.'

He picked the sledge up and walked to the door. 'It wasn't a box of chocolates was it?' he asked.

'Of course it was,' I said.

'Oh,' he said, in a very tiny voice, and went out.

It looked as if this Christmas was going to turn out to be one long string of disasters, until Marie Wood had the most amazing idea. She'd come out to show me her new Christmas dress, which didn't suit her at all, but she said she felt languid in it, and she asked Weird George to pull her down the street on the sledge. Suddenly she jumped off and he tilted forward into a snow drift.

'For goodness' sake!' she shouted. 'Haven't you kids got any sense at all? If you want Mr Punch to come here for his Christmas dinner, why don't you bring him on the sledge? Heck! Do I have to think of everything?'

It was, of course, the best idea she'd had in her life, and we were quite prepared to admit it. We all ran in and promised our mums we'd be back soon to lay the tables, and before they had time to object we were off.

The matron at the nursing home was first scandalised, and then greatly amused at Marie's suggestion. Mr Punch was ecstatic. He perched himself on the sledge with his arms tucked round his knees, and Matron wrapped a couple of blankets round him. She propped two carrier bags in front of him, and we could see that they were bulging with little parcels – bags and bags of sweets, I bet. George hauled the sledge along, as proud as if he was bringing home a prize catch of cod, and we pressed in close to the side to make sure he didn't roll off.

It was a bumpy ride, with Mr Punch bouncing about like a baby in a pram, and by the time we reached our street we were all hot and hungry. From the wonderful smell that greeted us you'd think that every oven door in the street had just been opened, and that every roast turkey was being taken out at the same time for a last basting to crisp them up for carving.

Mrs Finnigan's toes were steaming nicely in front of the fire, and she and Ganny were discovering a liking for my mum's rhubarb wine, and Fingers had brought his gravy to the boil, when they all stopped still. 'Vell!' said Ganny softly. 'Vot a racket!'

We'd been singing carols as we'd walked along, but our voices silenced as we reached the door. One tiny voice, bright as a diamond, came through:

> 'Away in a manger
> No crib for a bed,
> The little Lord Jesus . . . '

and rushed Fingers' thoughts back to the terrible groping darkness of the picture house.

'Crikey!' he whispered. 'He's back again!'

Mrs Finnigan's eyes dampened and fog clutched her voice. 'Will you just listen to that!' she smiled. 'You'd think it was some sort of angel singing!'

Ganny opened the door, when Robert's song had finished. She had never had carol singers at her door before, ever. Children spitting through her letter-box, scribbling dreadful things on her doorstep, dancing out of reach while she lunged at them; but never singing carols at her door. She saw Mr Punch beaming like a toothless imp at her from the sledge and she saw the bags piled high with sweets he'd spent his pension on. And as if in a dream she saw her pools money heaped up in the

bank, pounds and pounds and pounds of it, doing nothing. Wasted. Wasted. She didn't even know how much; but thousands, certainly.

'I von't tell them yet,' she thought, because the ideas in her head were scrabbling round like hamsters in a cage. Kevin helped Mr Punch off the sledge, and she closed the door behind them in the warm kitchen.

Later that Christmas afternoon things were obviously beginning to warm up in Ganny's house. Mums and Dads kept popping in for the glass of wine that Fingers promised them, steam clouded the window, and the talk and laughter of grown-ups rose and drifted with every opening and shutting of the door. We all stayed out in the street, taking turns on Ganny's sledge, tossing snowballs, and chewing. One by one the little ones heard about all the fun too, and as they ran across to us with their breaths dancing in front of them for their little bag of sweets they shouted through Ganny's letter box, 'Thank you Mr Punch! Happy Christmas!' I suppose we were making a bit of a noise. All of a sudden we saw Ganny at her window, struggling to get it open, and sticking her head through the top of it sideways, just as she used to do.

'Vot a terrible row!' she shouted. 'Vot you kids need is some place else to play.'

We were all shocked into silence.

'Anyway, you soon vill have, vether you like it or not. I've made quite sure of that. Crikey, I have!' We watched her yellow boil retreat, and saw the window close and the curtains being pulled across.

What was happening? Ganny turning nasty again – it seemed as if the wheel had turned full circle, and that we were back again to where we'd been in the summer. Ganny's door opened, and my mum came out. She stood in the doorway, arms folded against the cold, watching us.

'What Ganny means,' she said quietly, 'is that she's passed her savings on to me for our swimming pool fund. We've reached our target.'

You could have heard a sparrow breathe as Mum went back into the house and shut the door behind her. Then all of sudden the street was upside down with jumping bodies and whizzing snowballs and most of all with cheers that went up like bright balloons.

'Good old Ganny! Three cheers for Ganny Vitches! Hip hip hooray! Hip hip hooray! Hip hip *hooray!*'

* * *

But I suppose the last cheer of the day went to Weird George. Long after everyone had decided for the last time that they'd definitely had enough to drink, and had agreed that it hadn't been a bad Christmas after all, and had slipped off home to sleep it all off and to make room for Boxing Day, I saw George sneaking out of his house and across the road to Ganny's, with a brightly wrapped parcel under his arm. I met him at her door.

'What's that, George?'

'Ssh!' he said. He looked very worried. 'It's Ganny Vitches' Christmas present.'

I could see it wasn't the one I had given him for her. I squinted at the writing on the paper.

'But it says "To Darling George from your loving mother and father"', I pointed out.

'I haven't got any clean paper,' he muttered. 'And anyway, it's the present that counts.' He opened her door and went in; and I, of course, followed.

Ganny and Fingers were working out a jigsaw on the kitchen table, and Mrs Finnigan and Mr Punch were doing the washing-up. George plonked his parcel on top of all the straight edges that Ganny had lined up.

'Vat's this supposed to be?' she said, annoyed.

'A present,' George said gloomily.

'Good gracious, I can't be having any more excitement today, child. I'll be avake all night. I'll save it till tomorrow.' She pushed the parcel in the drawer of the table and carried on with the jigsaw.

'No!' shouted George. 'Don't do that! You have to open it now. It's a matter of life and death.'

'Crikey! It must be a bomb!' said Finnigan.

Ganny fished the parcel out and turned it over.

'Open it!' pleaded George.

'Shall I?' she asked the rest of us.

'I will if you won't,' Mrs Finnigan volunteered. 'I can't stand the suspense.'

Ganny took a knife from the drawer and very carefully eased up the sellotape. She prised up the creased wrapping paper and peered down the open end. Then she stared at George.

'D'you like it?' He beamed at her.

'I don't know. I can't tell vat it is,' she said. She turned the parcel round and just as slowly and carefully opened up the other end and peered down it, and stared up at George again.

'Well?' he asked.

'I don't know,' she said. 'I still can't tell vat it is. It's the same both ends.'

Impatiently George unwrapped the present for her.

'It's a stone!' Ganny said. 'A stone! Very nice!'

George turned the stone over. It had 'I am George's toytoyse' painted on it.

'A tortoise!' Ganny swallowed hard. She was struggling with her manners. Vat a lovely present. But it hasn't got a head, George.'

'He's asleep,' George whispered. 'It took me hours to find him.'

We all stared at the sleeping tortoise for a long time.

'D'you think he's a nice present?' George asked doubtfully.

'Oh, I do,' said Ganny. 'But I've no idea vat to do vith him.'

'I could come and take him for walks for you, when he wakes up,' George suggested.

Ganny looked a bit more cheerful.

'And if you like,' he went on, 'I could keep an eye on him till he does wake up.'

'That vould be kind,' said Ganny. 'I'm sure he vould be happier, vaking up in your house, vere he knows his vay round.'

'I'll take him back, then, shall I?' said George, greatly relieved. 'We don't want to upset him.'

'Righto!' Ganny nodded. 'You pop over sometimes and let me know how he's getting on.'

He nodded.

'And George . . . thank you,' said Ganny. 'He's a lovely Christmas present.'

George hung his head in embarrassment, shoved his tortoise in his pocket, and went back home.

And at last our most amazing Christmas Day had come to an end. The snow had stopped, and all the stars had poked their way through the dark sky. Kevin and Julie and I had taken Mr Punch home to the peace and quiet and plasticine smell of his pale green nursing home bedroom. Fingers Finnigan had walked his mother home in a pair of Wellington boots that my mum had found for her, and had hurried back to help Ganny search for missing jigsaw pieces, and to enjoy some of his cold turkey between hunks of Mrs Marriot's home-made bread. I watched the lights of the houses from my bedroom window, and saw Julie helping her mum put Matthew and David and Robert to bed. I saw George kiss his mum and dad goodnight, and maybe his tortoise too, before he drew his curtains. Marie's light came on, then Andrew's, and last of all a patterned square across the snow showed that Kevin had put his on too.

'What a bunch!' I thought. 'The best friends in the world!' I switched my own light off, and went to sleep.

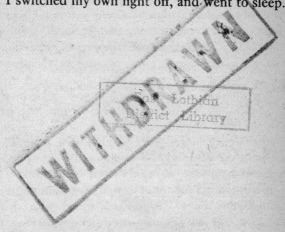
WITHDRAWN

East Lothian
District Library

OCTOPUS
Roy Brown

The Paxton Carnival takes place every year on the last Saturday in August. And every year the Brotherhood, a group of old comrades who had once graced the wrestling circuit, assemble in Harry Wilkin's dockside pub to organise the collection of money for a local charity.

It is decided that the money is to be sewn in black canvas bags, stitched into the shape of an octopus and transported on one of the carnival floats. But what the Brotherhood don't reckon on is the intervention of thieves, intent on spoiling the festivities, who take off with the octopus. And during a hair-raising police chase, pieces of octopus are scattered all over the dockland.

That's when Dusty Wilkins and his friends are roped in to recover the money. Eager and armed with their special knowledge of the area, their search leads to thrilling adventure and fun in the river, derelict houses, rubbish dump and disused railway. But the carnival is about to begin, time is quickly running out. Will they find the octopus before it's too late?

"Their adventures are described with gusto and a shrewd understanding of children. The speed and concrete detail of the narrative should commend it to young readers who will be carried away by the events."

Growing Point